Sunrise

'It is not flesh and blood but the heart which makes us Father and Son.'

- Johann Schiller

Email: bindisbooks@gmail.com

ISBN: 978-0-9943500-4-6

Any references to historical events, real people, or real places are used fictitiously. Names, characters, and locations are products of the author's imagination. Information cited is used to explain the story and the purpose of particular events to help the reader understand.

Front and back cover image by germancreative
Fivver: www.fiverr.com/germancreative

Interior book design by Belinda Topan

Artwork Created by Puppypaww

Twitter: twitter.com/puppypaww
Website: puppypaww.carrd.co/

Proof Reading and Editing was done by Sundus
Fivver Username: Sundus_writings
www.fiverr.com/sundus_writings

Ebook publishing with Ingramspark

First printing edition 2021.

www.belindatopan.com.au

Prologue

I remember her eyes. They were blue, like mine, hair blonde, shiny, like the sun. She always said I had hair like hers. Her smile, warm, and sweet. I remember how she held me close and sing me a lovely melody, rocking back and forth till my eyes felt heavy. Drifting into a deep slumber.

When was the last time I slept so well? Resting my weary body on a soft bed, closing my tired eyes, feeling safe in my surroundings and succumbing to unconscious. It's a being a long time since I embraced any of those comforts.

This is the life of the poor and abandoned, calling the streets our home and thieving our craft. Surviving. I have known so many people throughout the years, all killed by the hands of hunters and vampires alike. A missing slave gets more notice than the typical street beggar. No one in the upper class would bat an eye.

Gods, I am an idiot. I should have stayed away from the tavern, keeping my hands to myself. My self assurance and cockiness got me into this mess. I could have lasted another night, but now my time is almost up. Soon I will join the ranks of the dead.

Heavy footsteps bounce off the stone walls, echoing within the hollow cells, I am the only soul locked inside, listening to the rusted chains banning against each other, and hinges on the door loudly creak. I jolt awake from the smallest sound, my feet already on the ground, ready to run from the unsuspecting danger. My heart racing, pumping the adrenaline through my body.

The hunter brings a wooden bowl, with fat lining on top, filled with brown broth, bones, a bit of meat and organs swirling together. The smell made my stomach churn, bile rising into my mouth. I had to swallow it back down, remaining calm in front of the hunter. Grabbing the bowl from his hands, he huffs in approval and leaves me to my thoughts once more. I stare back at the contents, hoping to find the answers of the universe inside, half expecting an eyeball to rise to the surface of the broth and stare back at me.

So, this is it, my last hours. I sigh once more, putting the bowl down, ignoring the growl within my stomach. I may be hungry, but I am not desperate. I sit myself down on the cold stone floor in the corner, and the blazing colours of the setting sun tint the empty spaces red. Dusk will soon approach.

My stomach gurgles. If any louder, it would echo within the empty halls. Allowing all the hunters in the chambers to hear. *I am not touching that gruel.*

I'm ready. No longer will I have to thieve and sleep on the dirt grounds, running from hunters and vampires alike. The death may be slow and painful, but I would finally be free from this existence.

Death, I've danced this life for long enough, evading all your pursuits for my soul. Looks like we have finally reached our last dance. You finally have won, well done death.

The sun finally sets upon the horizon, and darkness shrouds the dungeons once more. The hunters clamber together, some holding ropes, another to unlock the door and two more to grab me. They act like I am a monster with so much security.

Let's hope it is quick.

An offer

Two posts stand in the centre of the courtyard, torches mounted on the top, providing the only source of light. Hunter's tie both arms to the two wooden posts, the rope digging into my wrists. I am left hanging like a piece of meat.

One hunter slowly brings out a carving knife. Slowly carving into my skin, slicing through my abdomen, my body burned throbbed as I slump against the ropes, my vision blurred, head throbbed, and warm sticky blood pooled out from me. Ringing a dinner bell for vampires. Hunters use their thirst as an advantage, capturing poor souls like me and bleed them out. After all, we are a pest to society. I'm lucky to live at this age, fighting, lying and cheating my way through.

It may have been a tough life, but a lonely one at that. It's true what the hunters say 'no one will miss me.'

We hear a low rumble from the shadows. Hunters prepare themselves for the battle, constantly looking over their shoulders. Vampires can see in the dark, humans can't.

I would be in a state of panic, but loss of feeling and light-headedness seem to prevent me the dread that is death. I don't care anymore, might as well die quickly and be a vampire's snack.
Several vampires launched themselves from the shadows. Barely able to keep my eyes open, I watch them come closer, claws out and hideously long incisors bared, snarling and charging for my blood. Unfortunately, two hunters notice their approach and kill them off. *So much for*

a quick death. The battle between hunters and vampires was short, not a single vampire remained, and no other dared to come any closer.

One hunter cut the ropes, and I helplessly fell to the cold, dirty ground with a thud. My body slightly ached on impact, but only intensified the wounds coming from my gullet. I feel more of my blood slowly bleed out from me. I cough a few times, struggling to breathe. My lungs fill with blood.

The hunters laughed and passed me by, ignoring my existence, ignoring my suffering.

With all the strength I have left, I pushed myself up and rolled on to my back. If I'm going to die, I rather die looking up at the stars. The stars always seem to comfort me; it's as if to say 'you're not alone.'

I stared at the sky, feeling my warm blood pooling out from me, and my body feeling numb. I'm closing in on death with each second. My vision slightly blurs, I blink a few times, hoping to have an unobstructed view of the stars when I die but that is quickly short-lived when a figure stands in the way of my gaze. I frown at the man, annoyed that he is in my view.

It took me a while to adjust to the darkness. As I notice his eyes are of a vampire, small black orbs stare back at my blue ones. *Has he not eaten in months?* Just when I thought I would die peacefully, a vampire comes along to snack on me. As long as I get to see the stars, I'll let him kill me.

The vampire kneeled down beside me and stares at me curiously, taking in the scene that lies before him.

Watching my blood bleed out me slowly, my eyes getting heavier, my breaths shallowing.

The vampire frowned and looks directly into my eyes. I could see the concern in them as he tries to decide what he should do next.

How funny, a vampire, that cares. Since when is that possible? They're heartless creatures, they don't care about their own, or us, only about themselves. So why does this one care?

The vampire moved closer and gently lifts my head, resting my body on his arm.

"I can save you," he offers. Save me? Meaning he'll turn me? Why? I'm a beggar, a human, I should mean nothing to a vampire, why would he give me a choice? I feel the grasp of death on my fingertips, and I don't have long to decide.

"Please," I rasp. Hoping the vampire heard my plea, I barely have any time left.

The Vampire nods, using his free arm, and bit his wrist. He let his own blood drip and places it over my mouth. I welcome the sweet liquid and drank deeply from the vampire's wrist. The vampire gently pulled away. He gazed at me with his lifeless eyes.

I felt strange, a numbing feel flowing through my body, dulling the pain, lulling me to go to sleep.

***

"Father, please!" I cry out to the man who stands in the grand hall. Allowing men to carry me out. "I won't

disappoint you again! I promise! Give me another chance!" I scream.

He held his hand up, and the guard stopped, only to keep me in place.

His heavy steps echo through the empty room, thundering as he walks closer towards me.

I am filled with relief as I watch the man I call my father coming over to give me one more chance.

He bends over, our eyes meeting. A Fiery look of disappointment and betrayal befalls him.

"You are no son of mine," he hisses. Moving away, he gives the orders to remove me.

I became like marble as the guards carried me away. A painful hole grows in my heart. Hope snatched away from me and I am left as a hallowed husk.

The First taste

I jolt awake, my body trembles. Feeling I am burning from the inside out, my throat dry, sore, everything ached. It hurts, everything hurts. I cover my ears, hearing a loud thrumming. I close my eyes, blinded by the bright sun streaming in from the window.

I clench my jaw. The horrible ache didn't ease feeling my teeth slice into my gums, and blood filling my mouth. It was old, bitter, and did little for the burn in my throat. I focus on the beating sound in my head, wanting to snuff the noise out and be in perfect silence. Cracking an eye open, I take in my surroundings.

Wrapped in cream sheets up to my torso, letting go of my head, I lift my old shirt up, still covered in my blood from the night they turned me. The wound gone, not a single scar found. I take in the room I am in, it's small but big enough for a wooden dresser and bed, with a wooden chair in the room's corner.

Carefully lifting the sheet, I gently shift off the mattress, my bare feet touching the wooden floor, my legs struggle to find the strength to stand me up, I stumble a bit before I can walk properly.

Carefully opening the door, I poke my head through the gap. No one, not even a mouse, is within the empty hall. Across from me are two doors are on the other side of each other. I hear the loud thumping from the door that is across from my room. I swallow the nonexistent spit. Hoping to dull the treacherous burn within. I tiptoe out the room into the empty hall. Reaching for the door on the other side. My hands shakily grasp the brass handle and turning the knob.

The thumping heard within increases in speed and the sweet smell intensifies. I push the door, swinging open to a bare room, nothing but a woman inside.

Squirming about on the wooden floor like a little worm, muffled squawks come through her gagged mouth. Limbs tied together, bruised and red from the thick, sturdy rope. Focusing on the loud thumping in her chest, drowning out her muffled cries. My breathing quickens, desperately wanting the heady scent to thrum through my empty lungs and drown my senses. Mouth dry, my throat parched, burning with every breath, I cannot stop. Gliding my tongue over the fangs, feeling the needed sharpness to carry out my next move.

It's all instinctive, I barely register my movements. The woman's muffled cries only fall on deaf ears, her heart only thrums faster, the yearning grows with disparity. My clawed hand reaches for her hair, pulling her up to her knees, baring her neck to me.

With unknowing strength, I tear her skin like paper and the red liquid pools out from the wound. It is a mere touch with my dry tongue, an explosion of flavour and pleasure rolls through me as I lap up the blood. I couldn't restrain myself any longer and desperately rip her into the skin with my fangs.

A satisfying muffled scream came from her as I gaped upon the sweet, life giving liquid within her veins. I drink faster, feeling the warm blood escape, smothering my mouth and into my clothes. I must not lose a single drop. A pleasant warmth spreads through my body, the burning sensation goes, and it only replaces with pleasure. *So good, so warm. Mine. Every drop is mine.*

A creak from the wooden door snaps me from my trance. Hearing an unknown voice sigh loudly and a foot thudding against the wooden floor. I tear away from my prey, snarling at the stranger. I will not let them take what's mine!

My sire stares at me blankly. He didn't react. Only stood in his place, and his bored expression sets in stone. His eyes stare into mine, searching, studying.

A presence becomes known in the air, a sharp instinct relays into my mind. *Stop, listen, respect.* I falter, the predatory instinct drains away. I close my eyes, trying to clear my head. I can feel it pounding into my mind.

Respect, bow. No! Resisting the presence looming over me, I focused back on what I started and finished the kill. I was less desperate and took my time, but it was only brief. Most of the blood was on me or the floor. I huff and let go of the corpse. I get up from the ground and stare at the vampire before me. The vampire who turned me. The bored look only turns into slight surprise, curiosity fills deep within his colourless eyes. *Odd.*

"Feeling better?" he asks me.

I notice the burn has only subsided. There wasn't enough. I lick my fangs, enjoying the sharp feel on my tongue. I want to kill again.

"Still hungry," I finally replied. The older vampire furrows his brow ever so slightly, staring at the ground in deep thought. He stays quiet before grunting quietly.

"I feared you would," he finally speaks and then sets his eyes back to me. "But you will have to wait. It is not safe to hunt yet," he finishes.

I scrunch my nose at him, growling shortly after, exposing a bit of fang at him.

"I don't want to wait, I want more," I hissed, taking a step forward. "I can't wait, I need it now," I add out of frustration. My mind buzzing with thoughts of tearing into tender throats, guzzling down sweet, warm blood, sating the burning desire within. My nature screams at me, hunt, kill, feed, over and over.

My sire only takes a step to the side, the bored expression never leaving. "Be my guest."

I waste no time reaching for the front door, swinging it wide open, inhaling the air, searching for the sweet aroma that will lead me to my next meal.

The world is a blur, my body moving without thought. Mindlessly searching, it is only when I hear the beating heart. I hunt down my target. Only the human exists and nothing else. Fear in the human's eyes and their heart picking up in pace.

My throat ignites, my fangs exposed, sharp and ready to puncture the throat of a helpless human. Excitement courses through me and a giddy delight leaps in my chest. Chasing down, pouncing and pinning the human to the ground. A wolfish smile grows. Showing off my long bloodstained canines. The human attempts to fight back are useless and pathetic. I chuckle at their plight before sinking down into their throat and tearing deep into their flesh. I groan, blood splashing onto my tongue, savouring the taste, not as desperate as the first kill. Fixated on the warmth pooling into my stomach, the sweet taste coating my tongue and throat. Their screams for help urge me on, glee rushing through as they slowly die down to whispers. The world around is irrelevant, it's just me and the kill -.

A flash of searing pain burns through my abdomen, bringing me back to reality. I let go of my meal, gagging in agony as I feel it dig through my body, I look down and see the tip of the blade protruding from my chest. *Fuck.*

"Disgusting creature!" the hunter snarls, pulling the blade out and kicking me down to the ground. Fear kicks into gear, I scramble to get away, unknown what to do in these situations. I can feel the blade stick into my abdomen, pinning to me the ground, I felt like a trapped lizard, my arms and legs flailing about, scraping on the stone street. "Die!" I embrace for the final blow, closing my eyes to the darkness, waiting for my subconscious to become nothing.

I hear a gag from above. The fresh, heady scent of blood fills my senses, snapping my eyes open to find the same hunter dead on the floor, with a hole in his chest and his heart laying next to him. I lick my lips, already eager to latch on and drink the rest. My mind blanks out, focusing on the taste, still bothered by the sharp object in my body.

"It's been a long time since I was a newborn," I hear the same monotone voice. They pull out the sword from my body. I felt the instant relief removed from my torso. "But you must understand you cannot just go after any human," my attention snaps back to my sire. I glare at the vampire as I keep drinking. "Or prefer to die next time?" he hisses. I let go with a satisfying sigh. Still hungry, but more in control of myself this time.

"Then what do you suggest," I croak, getting myself up from the ground, noticing the human I had attacked before slowly dying from blood loss. I wander over to finish the job.

"That you wait in the house and I bring you your food." I scrunch my nose in disgust and let go of the dead human, licking off the strands of blood from my face and fingers.

"Like a common dog," I hiss. My sire noticeably straightens himself, making him seem taller. He glares down at me, instincts take over, and I cower slightly at the older vampire. I mentally scold myself straight after.

"No, you are better than them. You're young and with today's display—lacking in control. Until you can contain yourself, I can teach you how to hunt and avoid hunters," he explains, kicking the heart that was torn out from the hunter's chest. I watch the organ bounce and roll down further into the empty street.

I relax a little, still staring at the heart, and lose myself in my thoughts. *What have I got to lose? It is unheard of—a sire looking after their child. They usually abandon them once they turn them and their fate is in the hands of the gods.*

"Why?" I ask with a whisper.

"Our species is going extinct, it's best if we try something different," he answers before turning away from me, "Now, are you coming or will you fend for yourself?" he asks me, his back still turned. I look at the mess before me, the urge to fight back and prove this vampire wrong, but something smaller and a little more persuasive tells me to follow, be smart, don't let my emotions take control. *I'll die out there, and he's my only hope.*

"Does my sire have a name?" I ask. He turns his head back to me, showing a small but soft smile.

"Syrus, you?"

"Rune."

Not everything living in the dark wants to kill you

I follow Syrus back to the city outskirts, unbeknownst to me how far I have run in such a short amount of time. I guess the stories are true, vampires have incredible speed. Already experienced wounds that would kill a mortal. The stab wound in my stomach has already healed. The super hearing enabling me to hear the beating hearts and voices from streets away. I stare at a bee and focus my attention, hearing the flutter of a bee's wings as they loom above the blooming flowers. What else is real? Super strength?

Syrus leads past the farmlands, reaching a banged-up two-story cabin on the outskirts of the woods. The roof looked broken, missing tiles and scattered pieces on the floor. Wooden planks to be missing on the wooden walls. stones missing from the chimney, black smoke escaping from them. I half expected the house to blow over in a powerful storm.

Syrus opens the door and allows himself in, I follow closely behind, and Syrus closes the door behind me. It looks nicer inside than it does on the out. It was clean, the floorboards still intact, working doors and fixed windows, the perfect illusion. The living space is compact. The fireplace sits to the far right of the room, still burning bright and hot. A small wooden chair sits in front of the fire, a pile of books neatly stacked up next to it on the wooden floor. The stair case is opposite of the fireplace, perfect symmetry of the room.

"Considering you painted yourself in blood, there's a hot bath waiting for you upstairs, the door next to your room at the end of the hall," Syrus concludes and sits in front of the fire. I look at my clothes and note the fresh and dried blood, mixed with dirt and grime. I can't think of a time when I last had a bath, there were times I stood in the icy rain. Feeling my toes and fingers go number, shivering as I desperatly try to clean myself. A hot bath, I couldn't help but feel a flutter of excitement in my chest and the threat of tears spilling from my eyes.

Step by step, I make my way up to the second floor, and sure enough, on Syrus's word, there was another door next to the room I had awakened in. *Why didn't I see that earlier?*

Opening the door, there in the middle was a tub, filled with scalding water, steam rising, filling the room with a light mist, a hint of chamomile and lavender lingers with the mist. Questions pop into my head. *When did Syrus have the time to draw him a bath? Where did he get the water?* Asking myself will never get the answers I need, so I decide to accept it and get in the bath.

The water felt hot, but it didn't scorch my skin as I expect it too, it felt pleasant feeling the heat. The warmth cocooning my body, feeling weightless in the water. It's so satisfying, it's been so long since I felt this. I only sink myself deeper till I'm submerged in the water. I enjoyed staying underneath, realising I no longer needed air and can stay under here for as long as I wish.

Coming back to the surface, wiping the water from my eyes. I see a cloth hanging on the side of the bath.

Ifrown at this rogue cloth, remembering not seeing one before.

Looking around the empty room, I can see no one. The door remained closed. Slowly, I reach for the cloth and begin washing the grime off my face. Enjoying the noticeable aroma of rose and the sound of water pour into the tub rings into my ears. I pull the rag away and skim the room again, still empty. I frown and begin the rest of my body. The water level has clearly risen since I stepped in. *Okay, I am going insane.* I ease myself back into the tub, trying to relax. Leaning my head backwards, washing my hair in scorching soapy water, scratching the grime out. *It's nothing Rune, it was always like this.*

I sit up again and scan the room and see a towel hanging on the doorknob. *That was not there before. Okay, time to get out.* I already deemed myself clean, but I had to cut my bathing experience short as random items appearing, and rising water is a little too much for me to handle. Stumbling to get out of the bath and wrapping the towel around me. I look for my clothes, scanning the place where I had left them initially. Gone.

I open the door and poke my head past the small crack, checking to see if anyone lingered in the halls. Once more not a single soul. Slowly creeping out, I walk back into my room. I find the bed neatly arranged with new, clean clothes, neatly folded on top of the covers. *Did Syrus do this?*

Shakily, I get changed into the clothes, and they fit well. They smell clean and soft. I stare down at myself, a smile creeping onto my face.

The light from the outside darkens as cloud black as midnight covers the midday sun, flashes of light emitted from the darkness, rumbling caused by the gods and then rain pouring down. I watch the rainfall slowly against the glass, hearing it bang upon the roof. It's nice to be on the other side of the elements, warm, clean, and inside a house with a sturdy roof above my head.

A wave of drowsiness crashes upon my body. Everything shut down, the brain no longer online and on autopilot, moving my feet to my bed. I gently grab the soft, warm garment. Gently rubbing my thumb against the fabric. *I barely remember the last time I laid in the bed.* I lift the cover and stare at the clean mattress. My stomach plummets thinking back to the dream I had before waking up. *My sleep controlled by nightmares.* I scrunch my nose in disgust.

Sitting on the bed, adjusting to the softness, bobbing myself up and down and enjoying the soft plushy feeling. But it was quickly dashed away with dread, drowned out by my inner thoughts, thinking back to that day. It has been so long since I last thought about that memory.

I wanted to resist the urge, but everything was out of my control, I fall back on to the bed, my head hitting the pillow, and the darkness overcomes me once more.

> *"Are – are you sure about this father?" I ask to stutter, standing in the centre of the pentagram. Shaking like a little lamb.*
> *"I am sure. This will work!" Father assures excitedly giving me ahead of a goat.*

I swallow and take a deep breath. Holding onto my breath, ignoring the foul stench of the blood.

Nightmares

My father, a few of his - friends? Followers? I don't remember what they were.

We travel deep within the mountains, rumours of an old tree sitting at its peak, protected by the harsh cold elements in a cave. I remember how odd it was for a tree to be growing in such a chilled atmosphere. How is it even growing in the dark?

Reaching the cave, hidden so delicately in the snow. It was dark, cold and wet, snow pouring into the hole. The wind howls through the hollow passage. My father lit a torch, slowly guiding us through the cave. Walking deeper and deeper, there it was. An enormous tree stands tall in the centre of the cavern. It leaves shimmering with beautiful, vibrant green, touched with a gold tinge.

The tree lit up the dark cavern like the sun's light. No longer did we need the torches. Life radiated from the tree itself. And just like all nightmares, the details haze out, skimming over the unnecessary plots and skip to the most crucial point of the story.

Standing before the tree, father had killed the adversaries on this trip, enchanting as he draws with their blood on the ground—another ritual and soon to be another failure. Father uses the rest of the blood to draw on the tree and draw marks on my face, still enchanting. The tree reacts to the spell. Markings glow, everything was so bright, it was blinding; I shield my eyes . . .

I wake up gasping once more, my body shakes, feeling my limbs wiggling my toes. If my heart could beat, it would sound like galloping horses, and I would work up a sweat as if I had competed in an Olympic sport. I scrunch myself up to a ball, ignoring the light of the moon beaming down into my room. Scrunching my eyes close and trying to force myself back to sleep . . . but I can't. Flashes of my memory play before me, forcing me to open my eyes yet again.

Sighing, I get out of bed, meandering down the steps. Syrus is in the same place as I initially left him, sitting in front of the chair, a book in hand and the warm glow from the fire, illuminating the room.

"How are you feeling?" I jump. I didn't expect him to know I was here. I didn't reply straight away, walking up to the older vampire and sitting on the wooden floorboards next to his small pile of books. I found the heat from the fire too much and scooted back a little. It felt like my skin was sizzling.

"I'm . . ." I stop to think. The hunger is only a dull ache, another human would snuff it out completely, but I am not desperate as I was when I first woke up. I can still feel the weariness in my body, I wish to sleep, but that will not be happening soon. "I'm a little hungry, but okay and sleepy," I murmur the last part, letting my eyes wander to the pile of books. *It has been a while since I had read something for pleasure, it mostly studies when I was younger.*

"Then why don't you go back to bed? It's natural for newly turned to sleep for a long time," Syrus explains, and I shake my head.

"No," I whisper. "Not yet," I grab one from the pile and open it to a random page.

"So you can read?" Syrus muses, still reading the page he is on. I glare at him, telling myself to ignore him, but the comment really got to me.

"I learnt at a young age," I retaliated, reading the book I had picked up. Syrus hums, a small smile gracing his lips.

"Would you like me to go get you someone?" he asks me. I stop and thought about it for a second, but shake my head.

"I can wait longer," I murmur, feeling my eyes getting heavier as I read. My body shifts to the left, little by little, I lean closer to Syrus. Subconsciously getting closer and closer, till my eyes closed, and I fell asleep leaning on him and his chair.

***

"Now since you can read, I want you to start reading all these books," my father declares carrying four heavy thick, leather-bound books, a heavy layer of dust covering them, my father drops the books, and a thick plume of dust wafts into the air. I sneeze over the books, and my father slaps me. "They're over a hundred years old, do you realise how precious they are!" he growls. I curl up in the seat and bow down.

"I'm sorry father," I murmur, tears threatening to spill from my eyes. Still feeling the sting on my cheek.

"Stop crying, you're a man and need to act like one," he huffs, opening the book to the first page. I struggle to read the passage. 'a guide to spells.'

"What if I can't understand certain words," I whimper, curling into the chair, shutting my eyes, waiting for him to explode at me.

"Come and get me and I will help, but until then, I don't want you leaving this room till you have read all of those books," he demands and slams the two oak doors shut, the clash echos loudly within the personal library.

I jump awake once more, shakily swallowing the non-existent spit from my mouth and my hands judder. I look around to find myself back in my room. The sun blaring down. I could feel incisors push against my gums, slicing into my tongue. Everything burns within my body. *Blood, need blood.* I hear the familiar thumping outside my room and across the hall. Rushing out of the bed and stumbling to the door. Nearly tripping over my feet to reach the doorknob and ripping the door open. Lunging at my captured prey, I waste no time biting into their soft flesh and focus all my attention on the warmth pooling into my stomach. Feeling the fire doused throughout my body. I moan deeply as I continue to drink and enjoy the feeling of pleasure crash down. I let go of the body, feeling a little more refreshed but still hungry. One is never enough.

"I had a feeling you would be hungry," Syrus's voice grabs my attention. Another human in his grasp, fighting with all their might to get out from it. Syrus rolls his eyes, at their attempts and throws them to me, capturing them in mere seconds and feed.

I finished them off quickly just as I did with the first one, feeling better, more in control of myself. "Sleep well?" Syrus inquires leaning against the door frame. I go to open my mouth but think back on the dreams, my insides churned and quaked, fear lingers in the back of my mind, taunting me. Syrus takes note of my silence. "You passed out on the floor, I took you back to your bed if you were wondering." I wasn't, but I believe he was trying to change the subject.

"Thank you," I whisper, getting up from the floor. Syrus sighs a little and leaves the room, only to come back with a rag in his hand.

"When you feed do you go to the artery or anywhere on the neck?" he asks and gives me the rag. I take it in silence and wipe my face and shrug in response. "I don't see the difference, I get blood in the end."

Syrus walks over to the body, inspecting my bite, frowning as he does, and shows me the gouge I tore into the shoulder.

"You need to aim for the throat," he points. "There's an artery you can tap into, you can drink without making a mess and getting the most from the body." Syrus's fingernail sharpens, slicing into the skin, showing me where I need to bite. "It takes practise, but when you're able to be more in control, you can feel for it," he murmurs dropping the body.

"How long will it take?" I ask.

"Give it three months, and you will have some semblance of self when hunting, for now, it's not possible," Syrus explains. "But focus on the throat if you can, don't fret too much if you forget, I know how maddening the hunger is." I nod at his words staring at my feet, feeling a little defeated but can't help the fear lingering in the back of my head, feeling heavy-hearted in my chest. "Are . . .

are you all right?" Syrus asks a little softly. I look up at the vampire, staring into his light grey eyes and nod, swallowing the lump in my throat.

"Yeah, just . . . tired," I lied and walked out of the room, leaving my sire behind.

***

"No, no, no," my father huffs, stomping over to me, nostrils flaring, eyes burning as he stands over me. "You are doing it wrong, you stupid boy," he hisses.

"I... I . . . I" I stutter trying to explain myself. "I did the best I c-could," I stutter shrinking under him.

"No, you're not," he hisses, grabbing my arm, dragging me down the halls and throws me back into the library. "Do not come out till you have finished reading all those books again!"

Growing Pains

I have grown restless in the last two weeks, unable to go anywhere into the city, only able to wander in the forest nearby. It's only becoming more frustrating as I fall asleep at random intervals, there have numerous places Syrus has found me sleeping and the in the forest was the latest one. It not my proudest moment but the nightmares haven't delayed either, I feel more and tired as the days go by. Feeling my energy being sapped away from my past. It's haunting.

I feel like someone else is in control of my body, always hungry and sleepy. There are only a few brief hours where I feel like I am in control, and I hate it.

I'm currently lying on the wooden floor, glaring up at the ceiling, Syrus has given me the kindness to move his chair and read in the room's corner, letting me wallow in self-pity.

"When will this end?" I murmur to myself, hoping Syrus would spark a conversation with me. He's an odd vampire, he spends his days reading and catching humans for me to feed, like clockwork, he knows when I am about to nuts with the bloodlust. What I found most strange about Syrus is his eyes, it's unnerving to have white, and black dots stare back at you. When I think about it, not once have I seen him feed, has been eating or is he just giving his prey away to me? Remembering I looked at my reflection and seeing my eyes have changed, red pupils slit like a cat's eye. I look at Syrus again, still reading, haven't noticed my comment. I swallow the fear and open my mouth once again. "When could you gain control of your hunger?"

Syrus twitches in acknowledgment, his eyes still reading the book but a slight frown form on his brow.

"I don't remember," he rasps, clearing his throat straight after. "It has been - a long time since I turned," he pauses solely keeping his focus on the book in front of him.

"But I want to be in control now," I whine, frustration bubbles up from dark depths.

"Give it time, it's only been two weeks," he assures, but this only added more fuel to the fire. I feel out of control of my body everything is still so new and weird, I hate it, I want to be back to normal, I want to hunt at my leisure, I want to sleep when I want to sleep, I want these goddamn nightmares to go!

"I don't have time," I hiss, feeling my fangs extend. "I want to hunt when I want too, I want to go into the city, I want to be out of this house!" I shout to the roof.

"And die by hunters? Be my guest," Syrus replies monotonous. I sit up, growling at the older vampire, baring my fangs at him.

"I don't want to die, I want you to teach me, or let me hunt!" I hiss. Syrus sighs carefully placing the bookmark between the pages and closes the leather-bound book.

"You are in no control to learn anything," he calmly responds.

"Who says I had to listen to you anyway," I huff.

"May I remind you of the incident that occurred two weeks ago?" Syrus hisses, his eyes spoke the rage of a thousand men burning within his eyes. I couldn't help but shudder under his gaze, but fight back the urge to curl into a ball and stand my ground as the vampire steps closer to me.

"I'm tired of listening to you, I want to eat," I hiss.

"You will eat when it is night, but it is broad daylight, it is not safe," Syrus growls, showing a bit of fang afterwards.

"Try to stop me," I challenge. Syrus straightens his back, his nostrils flare, hands twitch, ready for me to make a move.

Moving to the front door, reaching for the handle. I swept off feet, fingertips just brushing the metal before I hit the ground. My head hitting the floor, Syrus's hand grasping my throat and pushing me into the boards, snapping like twigs under the amount of force. Syrus bares fangs at me, like a viper ready to strike. Blind rage courses through the older vampire, his clawed hand slowly slicing into my flesh. Instinctively, I bare my fangs in return. We stare down at each other, not once daring to look away. A battle of wills, who would win.

"If you want to throw your life away, go-ahead. I thought you would have learnt your lesson by now," Syrus growls, letting go of my throat. Slowly sitting up, my hand flies up to my throat, inspecting the skin to remain sliced up. But thankfully it had healed. "You cannot be aware of your surroundings. You have noticed, haven't you?" I flinch at his words, acknowledging what he meant.

"Can't you just be on watch or something? I feel so, so pathetic," I whimper, pulling my legs up to my chest, my fangs still out. I feel like a crybaby. Never did I behave like this when I was human.

"I can, yes, but there are more hunters than there is us, I need you to be aware of your surroundings," Syrus reasons.

"I'm always aware of your presence. Like a little voice telling me to respect you, to listen to you," I murmur into my knees, feeling the tears well up.

Syrus notes the tremble in my voice. Taking a deep breath, slowly he crouches to my level and sits on the floor next to me.

"I guess we can try to hunt tonight," he compromises. "Hunters have difficulty seeing then," Syrus adds and I nod in agreement, wiping the stray tear away.

"I agree."

***

It's harder than I expected. There are so many smells mixing. It's like my favourite bouquet put together or my favourite meal and laid out before me. Hunger rises deep within my gullet. So many sounds of pulsing hearts, and old blood, all inside, protected by their stone walls. I wanted to break in and feed on them while they slept. Syrus clapped his hand on my shoulder, jolting me out from my thoughts. He looks down at me with a knowing look. I hung my head, remembering the look from my father. Disappointment.

It's hard to remain in control right now, so much is overwhelming my senses, unable to keep them in check as there are a plethora of humans in this city. Sleeping soundly in the night, with their lulling heartbeats. The burn in my throat ignites tenfold, my fangs out and ready to strike.

A warm, heady scent lingers in the air, my mind switches off, a growl rumbling in my chest, the hunger won. Nothing mattered except the blood and my desire to feed. Syrus calls my name, I hear him screaming for me to stop but it was too late. Following the scent, desperate to sate the burning fire within, I am back at the courtyard that started all of this.

A human tied to two familiar posts bleeding out. More vampires appeared by my side, and a sense of urgency grew. The kill was going to be mine. We were all desperate for blood, fighting each other to get to one human. Hunters use this opportunity to pick them off, one by one. So focused to getting to my prey, I barely stopped the hunter piercing me with his iron sword. I snarl at the hunter. My frustration for the kill grew stronger. I would let no one stop me.

A sharp stabbing pain hits me in the side of my skull and everything went black. Falling to the ground, I couldn't move, and unable to fight back. My skull pounded, throbbing. The intrusion I could feel in my head is heavy. Numbness took over, I struggled to function my body. Forcing my arm to move and grasp the invasion in my skull and tearing it out from my brain. Feeling fingers again, my vision gradually returning, I felt the sudden relief and stare at the arrow in hand, coated in my blood. Everything in me reconnected and heal as soon as I removed the arrow.

I looked around to find bodies of vampires and hunters lay dead. Mangled mostly, throats torn and ripped apart, vampires' heads cleanly cut off. Syrus in the centre of it all, lost in the bloodlust as he drinks from the hunter's neck. Blood coating his mouth, clothes and fingers, deep in the colour red. He lets go with a satisfied sigh, dropping the last hunter to the ground, fear spikes in the back of my spine as I stare into my sire's bright red eyes, the look of a deadly predator willing to kill anything that gets in his way.

Slowly he steps towards me, his eyes trained on me as I desperately try to move, and stumble over my feet. I knew I screwed up, and I said I wouldn't. I shake before the vampire, shutting my eyes as he draws near. Waiting for my punishment.

His hand gently plops on my head. "See, told you weren't ready."

I snap open my eyes in surprise. Syrus kneeled before me, his clawed hand gently laying on my head, the predator no longer there, the Syrus I know has returned. I shake still, surprised by this sudden change in mood.

"Y-you're not mad?" I stutter, Syrus frowns and shakes his head.

"No," he replies, calm. "I had a feeling this would happen," he removes his hand and sighs. "Are you all right? The arrow that pierced your head knocked you out for a bit," he asks I nod my head still shaking. Waiting for some kind of punishment. This always happened when I mess up. "Good, I left the human tied up for you, if you are still hungry," he says haphazardly and stands up, giving me his hand. I gently take it, and Syrus help me up on my feet. I shake and lose my footing, falling onto him, leaning in for support.

"Did you kill them all yourself? I ask, getting a better look from above.

"They were going to kill you," Syrus answers as he looks at the disarray of bodies strewn across the street.

"I'm s-sorry," I whisper feeling the tears streak down my face, shaking in his grasp. Syrus frowns at me, not understanding why I was shaking in his hold. Syrus gently let's go, gazing into my eyes.

"It's all right, I expected this," he assures me, and I shake my head.

"I should have been in control, I should have listened to you when you called my name, I should have done -." I cut myself off when Syrus put his hand on my head again, bracing for some kind of punishment.

"Don't beat yourself up. We all make mistakes, we all learn from them. You can't control yourself, and it will be awhile before you have a sense of anything," Syrus soothes, his voice soft but firm. I tremble under his hand, not able to able to take this kindness, this understanding. He was so cold before what changed. I swallow the lump down my throat, wiping the wet tears from my eyes. Syrus removes his hand once more and gives a small smile. "Now, are you going to eat?" he asks me, moving out of the way, and the human comes to my view. I feel the burning ignite in my throat, nodding to his question.

Knowledge is power

I take time to wander the halls of my home, getting lost within the infinite number of rooms, always seem to shift, with each door I open, swearing I have already been here and as I continue to wander, I always end back in the same place—the library. Heaving a deep sigh, I make my way back to my seat and force myself to re-read over the potion recipes. Though it lasted for a few seconds and my eyes wander over the portrait of the woman with long, straight golden hair, bright blue eyes, skin like snow.

"Mother, do you think Father would have been kinder if you were still here?" I asked the portrait, secretly hoping for an answer.

I open my eyes, surrounded by darkness once more. Feeling the aching deep within my chest, hollowed and heavy, unable to heal. I want to rip my heart out just to stop the ache. It is a permanent solution, but I am not willing to go to such extreme lengths. *It had been a long time since I have thought of her.* I sit myself up, contemplating to get out from the warm covers and steal another book from Syrus downstairs. Still able to see, I am no longer afraid to be in the shadows. I feel more at ease to be in them.

I hear a knock at the door, freezing in my bed, and wait for a response. "Rune, you awake?"

I ease a little, nodding at the door but realising Syrus can't see me through the door. "Ah, yes. Come in."

Syrus comes in, carrying a book in his hand. A small smile graces his lips, Syrus stands at the doorway.

"Grab your shoes, we have little time," he urges. I get out of bed, confused at the sudden urgency.

"What's going on? Did the hunters find us?" I asked, tripping over my own two feet as I rush to get to my shoes. Syrus shakes his head in response. The smile hasn't left as he watches me struggle to get my shoes on, amused by my panicked dexterity he patiently waits till I get on them on my feet.

"No, nothing like that, but we still need to hurry," Syrus urges. I stumble to my feet and follow the older vampire outside of our home. Quickly running through the forest, deers, rabbits all run out of the way, afraid to be our next meal, but we found no interest in eating them. Syrus leads me past the forest, reaching the other side of the clearing. A large hill stands before us and Syrus wastes no time climbing up. We are only halfway, still rushing to get to the top. If I was human, I would huff and puff, and collapse onto the ground, dying from exhaustion.

Thinking back over the month since Syrus and I had our small heart to heart. Nothing hasn't changed between us, other than my constant push to be good at hunting. I have accepted to sit back and let the food come to me, till I can gain some control.

The weird events of the bath only happened once, never again did those odd occurrences happened. I never brought it up with the vampire, I didn't want to seem like I was crazy. Yet he seemed to know something, telling me all items for future baths are in the room. Definitely odd.

As for time, it is on my side, finding books a simple escape to pass it, it differs from the grimoires I used to read. Kept in a perfect bubble of ignorance, not knowing the outside world but here in my two hands. Syrus has noted my awe as I am deeply ingrained in his small pile of finished books. Bringing more and more from the confined spaces of his room to the living area downstairs. Silently encouraging me to read more.

One book is the history of Rome, written by an old scholar. In another are the tales of the Greek gods—I feel like everyone's problem would be less if Zeus kept it in his pants. Thoughts and philosophy, and ramblings of those who considered a heretic or a madman. Science, math, and languages I am foreign with. I yearn to learn what they inscribe within these pages, I yet to have the courage to ask Syrus to teach me. Math is another hard one, unable to grasp the formulas, understanding their use but unable to know where the numbers come from. I feel like I can learn more from the older vampire, unsure how long he has been wondering about this earth. I know he would have the answers I need.

Finally reaching the top, I plop myself onto the ground, staring up at the starlit sky, in awe of the colours and twinkling lights. It's peaceful up here, feeling the cool breeze against my skin, the calm serenity the nightlife brings and the stars glistening the ink sky and the grass pricking beneath my skin. My jaw drops open as a beam of light shoots across the sky, then another, and another, till the sky fills with them, all-dancing across inky glittering mess.

"It's a meteor shower," Syrus whispers as he watches the sky with me.

"Is that why you brought me out here?" I asked him, sitting myself up from the ground. Syrus nods and passes me the book he carries in his hand.

"I stumbled upon this book when I was in the city. The author talked about an array of lights shooting across the sky. Looking into it, he found a few accounts happening every few hundred years. We are lucky it's happening this year," Syrus chuckles as I read the passage he was talking about.

"Can you—teach me what you know," I ask him, gently closing the book. Syrus was a little surprised, but eased a little.

"What is it you are struggling with?" I wince a little. The idea of me struggling to learn it only brings back many terrible memories.

"Math, and a few other things," I grumble, curling myself up into a ball.

"Math can be tricky," Syrus muses. "I can teach you what I know, but I won't be able to answer everything," he shrugs. I frown at the vampire, uncurling myself.

"I thought you knew everything," I state and Syrus laughs. For the first time, he laughs an actual, genuine laugh.

"No, definitely not. I may be old, but I don't know everything. Only those with arrogance would claim such a title," Syrus smiles. I think back to my father, he held such an air of arrogance about him, walking around like he was a gift from God, many of our community would flock to him for answers, even if my father was wrong, he would say it was a test. He put the same pressures onto me, expecting me to know all there is to do with magic and get every spell right in one go, regardless if I had read the books only once. "Let me give you some advice, your choice to take it," Syrus continues as he snaps me from my thoughts. "Never stop learning. The world is always changing, and as man continues forward, we will learn more and more when time goes on. We have time on our side, we do not have an excuse to stop learning. Knowledge is power but never fall to arrogance, that is a trap for anyone who seeks in pursuing knowledge. Always act as if you know nothing in the world, and you will always find your answers."

I am left in awe. Something about Syrus's words moved me. It is a different view to look at the world, something that is unheard of, to treat the world as if I know nothing, instead expected to know everything. I feel less pressured, more at ease with the pace I am going at. No one is expecting anything of me. Syrus expects nothing. I feel like I can breathe again—not that I need to. I feel my throat tighten, tears slowly trickle from the sides of my eyes. Syrus takes note, unsure whether to put his hand on my shoulder, deciding against it and put his hand away and asks. "Are you all right?"

"Y-yeah," I sniffle. "I just heard no one say that to me before," I whisper, curling up again, into a protective little ball. To be so vulnerable like this, it's agonising. I wanted no one to see this side of me.

"I gathered. The nightmares haven't stopped either," Syrus returns to his sullen features, looking a little sadder than his monotonous voice.

"How?"

"You talk in your sleep. You're always pleading to try harder and get better." My chest tightens, I clench my jaw and shut my eyes as the memories flash before me. "You don't have to tell me anything. Just know, I'm nothing like the person you are dealing with in your dreams," Syrus assures.

"Promise?" I whisper, hugging my knees closer to my chest.

"I promise."

What is this feeling?

"You did well but make sure you enunciate the word, by opening your mouth a little wider, you'll be able to get the sound when you pronounce it," Syrus explains. Opening his own mouth wider as he pronounces the said word, emphasising the mouth movements. I nod, feeling already drained from the small hours putting into a single word and then stringing sentences together. My throat burn as if I have swallowed flames from the fire and head drooping to one side, finding the wooden floor looking ever so comfy, like it's made of a soft pillow. Syrus sighs and snaps the book shut, jolting me from my daze. He gives a small chuckle before getting up from his seat and putting the book away. "I think that's enough for one day." He hums.

"Yeah - sounds good," I yawn, resisting the urge to close my eyes. Desperately knowing what is on the other end. "Actually—I can keep learning, I'm fine," I murmur, finding an excuse to stay awake. Syrus raises an eyebrow at me, questioning my sudden change. *How do you do that? Can I raise an eyebrow like that?* Subconsciously, I contort my face, trying to mimic Syrus's look. Syrus eases himself back into his seat, eyes gazing into mine. I felt uncomfortable under his gaze, shrinking a little, feeling the fear creep up my spine.

"Your eyes are grey, you're not concentrating and I can see you leaning towards the floor," Syrus notes my behaviour. "I do plan to get someone for you to eat, if you can stay awake, it wouldn't be too long," Syrus concludes, and I feverishly nod my head. Staring back into his own eyes once more, also noticing the whites in them, the colour nearly gone.

"Have you been eating?" this caught him off guard. Syrus sits back before getting up and heading to the door. He stops and turns to me. His mouth slightly open, wanting to speak, say something. He noticeably takes a breath.

"I—It's not important, you eating, is." That is all he said and leaves the house. I couldn't help but feel as if I hit a sore spot. I felt ashamed to ask, guilty even, I didn't expect to get such an adverse reaction from the older vampire. Feeling the heavyweight in my chest, I look back to the small bookshelf, searching through the small selection, hoping to distract myself for a little longer.

Syrus's attention to detail is incredibly scary, noting my attempts to forego sleeping, using any excuse I can before collapsing to exhaustion. Not once did Syrus call me out for it, nor did he scold me, he just let me run my course. He's patient, cautious, keeping his distance when possible, but then it breaks. This wall he has put up, I see it crumble from time to time, enjoying the small conversations, going off-topic during my lesson, an eager but kiddish excitement grows within him as he shows me something new and pride. I see it, in small glimpses when I get a math problem right, a language I can understand—even if it is little words, teaching me the wonders of the stars and the religions of old and new, I can see it—more than I have ever seen before my life on the streets.

The ache in my chest only grew as a dull pain intensifies, lingering up to my throat. The warm salty tears leak from the corner of my eyes, knees give way, and I am on the floor sobbing. So much buried emotion lingering beneath my chest, digging deep within to make sure I never felt it again. Having no time to reflect, no time to think of the past. I had to survive. I had to live, even if it was hell, and if I died by the hands of a vampire or by law, I accepted it. As a human, I had nothing, and I had accepted my fate.

Wiping away the tears, trying to gather my thoughts. Letting all the bad feelings and memories swirl together like a dangerous liqueur. Everything hurt, physically and emotionally. *Remember, mother's words, breathe Rune, focus on the world around you.* A technique my mother taught me when I was young, I was so little, only three. Father always hated when I cried, I made too much noise. *What do you hear?* I hear her voice whisper in my head. I focus on the outside world. I hear the forest, the birds singing, the water flowing through the stream. I hear footsteps. Coming closer, heartbeats loud and clear, the fire blazed within my body. The smell of toxins and the sound of metal clanging together, the sounds of a horse neigh and the foul stench of animal blood overriding my senses. *Hunters!*

My eyes snap open, and they kick the door down, I quickly get to my feet, feeling the points of my fingers sharpen to claws. Charging at the hunters with full speed, I only sliced the throat of the first hunter before arrows fly in, their pointed ends sticking into my body. I froze in shock, feeling the pain agonisingly go through my body. They quickly swarm in using this chance to tie me up, swords sticking into me for good measure. Small amounts of blood leaked through the wounds, my body desperate for more blood.

A hunter brought his sword close to my neck, sizing the swing before lifting his arm up. I close my eyes, begging Syrus to appear out of nowhere.

"Keep em' alive," I open one eye and the head hunter waltzes in. "There's another one, and he's very protective of this leech." I glare at the hunter, baring my fangs at him.

"We have our orders, Daniel," the one with the sword grunts.

"Does it look like I care? They all deserve to die, no harm in keeping em' alive till we get the other one," he signals the men to move me out, getting a sack and putting it over my head and feeling something massive hit me at the back of my skull.

***

"Wakey, wakey," I hear the same voice again, and I am splashed with water. I shake myself awake, my eyes scattering around the room, trying to gather my bearings, understanding where I am. I recognise the stained glass, the wooden pews, the podium and the cross sitting before me. On the stone steps, I snarl at the hunter named Daniel. He grins as he walks closer to me and grabbing the back of my head.

"You've caused a lot of trouble for me," he laughs, shaking his head, and lets go of my hair. "The city is in panic, fewer vampires on the streets, more—clever ones popping up, like a following of some sorts, and it's all because of him," Daniel explains before swiping me across the face. "If you just laid down and accepted your fate, we wouldn't have issues like this," he grunts and unsheathes his sword. "So let's see if he cares, huh!" he shouts and his voices echos within the church. "Only the Lord can judge, sending you creatures back to the fiery hole you once came from, knowing they will embrace me with open arms from god himself." I watch in silence as the vampire hunter soaks in the cross before him, feeling the pride burning within.

I growl at the hunter, feeling my stomach churn and feel the bile rise in my throat.

Daniel didn't take kindly to my growl, quickly swinging another punch in my face. I spit out the precious blood filling my mouth, a smile slowly creeping upon my face.

"He'll slaughter you when he finds us," I snicker. I can't wait to watch him tear him from limb, hearing them beg for their lives, screaming in agony as Syrus destroys them. The hunter felt uneasy as he looks my feral grin, taking a step back from the psychotic vampire.

"Let's just kill you now then," Daniel finding his spine once more, getting his sword at the ready but it was already too late. The beautiful smell of human blood paints the air. A guttural groan escapes my lips as I wish to lap up every drop of blood that is spilt.

Screams come from the outside, all pleading and begging to come in as they bang against the wooden doors. Daniel gives a new shade of white as he hears his men scream and become strangled cries before dulling to nothing.

"You sure you can take him on?" I mock the hunter, grinning from ear to ear. Before Daniel even reacts, the doors slowly creak open, hauntingly echo between these stone walls. Syrus slowly walks down the aisle, blood coating his hands and mouth. His eyes still hauntingly grey but soon will be red as the blood of his enemies.

Daniel trips over his feet and quivers as Syrus towers over him, his clawed hand grasping his throat, slowly lifting him from the ground, Daniel's legs dangle in the air, hands clenching Syrus's arm, his face slowly going red from the lack of air.

"Tell me," Syrus whispers. "How were you going to kill me?" he asks Daniel and digs his claws into the throat, tearing it out his windpipe, blood painting the stone floors. I lurch forward, desperate to lap up all the blood. I hear Syrus sigh and cut me loose, and stopping myself from drinking any more blood from the floor. "I really can't leave you alone for five minutes, can't I," he muses. I give him a smile and shrug.

"They found us," I croak, Syrus's smile disappears.

"I know, I'm sorry I should have been more careful," he apologises, and I shake my head.

"It's okay, no one could have predicted this," Syrus sighs and stands up.

"Can you walk?" he asks me, and I try to stand on my own two feet before falling back down. "I'll take that as a no," he chuckles and picks me up, carrying me outside the church. I look at his eyes, no longer the terrifying white but is still grey.

"Have you eaten enough?" I ask him while he carries me in his arms. For the first time, I felt safe to be in the city. As long as I am with Syrus, I know I will be all right.

"I have," he answers.

"Liar," I murmur, feeling exhaustion wash over me. Syrus stays silent for a while, walking through the streets to the outskirts of the town. I notice we are heading in the wrong direction. I guess our home isn't safe anymore.

"I rarely eat," Syrus admits. I feel my eyes getting heavier.

"Why? Don't like blood?" I ask, not that it would be possible, it tastes fantastic. Syrus lets out a throaty laugh.

"No, I like it, and the feeling when you kill, something that is programmed into us as we wake as vampires," he explains. "I don't eat because - well, I had nothing to live for," he explains, I drowsily frown, trying to make sense of all this in my sleepy state.

"How long have you been doing this?" I ask him, and I hear him hum.

"Roughly five hundred years."

"What!?"

Home is where the heart is

Syrus carries me out of the city, letting me rest in his arms as I slowly heal from my injuries. I can feel the hunger getting worse as Syrus wanders aimlessly. I think over our recent conversation, still surprised to discover the vampire's age. Five hundred years. No wonder he knows so much, he's lived through it all. I wonder if I could last that long? Still, I wonder what changed his mind. Why did he turn me? If he hated life so much, why would turning me make a difference? I wanted to ask, learn his reasoning, but it also scares a part of me. He intended to turn me, teach me till I can look after myself—will he leave once I can?

"Got a destination in mind?" I rasp, drowsily looking up at the sky, admiring the stars.

"I do, but it will be awhile before we get there," he murmurs, still focused on the road before him. I nod, feeling the insatiable hunger gnawing at my sanity.

"I'm hungry," I whisper.

"There's a village close by, maybe we can find a place there," Syrus smiles. I smile and nod, feeling another wave of drowsiness crash down upon me.

"Syrus," I whisper, I hear a hum as a response. "Why did you turn me?" I ask sleepily. He stops and stands in the middle of the road like a frightened deer, ready to flee at a moment's notice. He looks down at me and then to the road. Syrus furrows his brow, trying to understand his own reasoning.

He continues walking and opens his mouth. "Why do you ask?"

"You said you had no reason to live, why now, why me?" I can feel my eyelids get heavier at each second. Syrus nods his head slowly and looks at me softly.

"There are two reasons," he answers. "I turned you because I saw a boy helpless. Unable to fight back the hand the universe had dealt him. I saw something about me, in you. Selfish as it sounds, I just wanted to turn you so you could have a second chance," Syrus begins.

"And the second?" I croak.

"I couldn't let you die," Syrus hisses. "Sacrificed, to lure a bunch of ferals, it's disgusting," Syrus growls to himself, baring his fangs to the dirt road before relaxing, letting out a huff of air.

"And I've nearly gotten myself killed three times already in the space of two months. Our home destroyed, argued with you," I list all the unfortunate happenings, feeling like I am a burden to this vampire. "It's almost the universe is still out to get me," I joke to lighten the mood, but I know deep down, that is genuinely how I feel. A burden to those who take me in, leaving me alone in this world. *I don't want to be alone, I want a family, a family who loves me, for who I am and what I can do. No longer do I want to be alone.*

"Twice, the third was mine, I should have been more careful." Syrus berates, snapping me from my thoughts. "Our home doesn't matter, things are replaceable, lives aren't, your life is more important than my belongings. As for the arguing, it would be nice if it happened less, but its expected. I am nothing but a stranger to you. So no, you're not a burden," Syrus rectifies. I felt at ease, assured that I am not to blame, even if my brain is telling me otherwise. In the back, it screams I am in the way.

"Why do you care so much?" I ask, feeling the small tears leak from my eyes. Syrus stays silent, eyes focused on the path before him.

"I—can't exactly explain it - I care cause I want you to live and see you be able to survive on your own. I also enjoy getting to know you, teaching you about the world, I feel like I have a reason again. Could have turned anyone, but something told me, it had to be you - creepy as that sounds." I huff out a laugh and shrug.

"No, it makes sense, it's like a little voice whispering the back of the head. I've heard it, tells me to respect you, I ignore it though it's annoying." Syrus tenses, visibly swallowing.

"Good, keep ignoring it, respect is earned, not given."

"Eh, your doom and gloom could use some work. You could have talked to me more in the first couple of weeks," I tease and Syrus lets out a chuckle.

"I didn't know what to say, I haven't interacted with anyone for centuries," Syrus defends himself.

"Yeah, but you could have done something, instead of reading your little books," I argue back.

"So could you, but you were too stubborn to say anything, walking around like you didn't need anyone," Syrus sniggers. I bit my tongue, knowing we were just going to end up in circles, rectifying our actions toward each other. Syrus smiles down at me and shakes his head.

"Okay, we got off the wrong foot, so how about in future we are kinder, open up a little more, so things aren't so-," I trail off to find the right words.

"Weird, odd, hostile?" Syrus prompts and I shrug my shoulders.

"Whatever works," I say, looking back at the inky sky, filled with the glittering lights. "What do you think? Truce?"

"I thought we had one when I began teaching you?" Syrus teases.

"We do, but I want to know more about the vampire who turned me. Five hundred years of existing, and you don't get to leave without telling me anything," I point out. Syrus's smile lessens but is still there, going deep in thought, I can see his eyes have glazed over, lost deep into the depths of his mind.

"That is fair, but it goes the same for you," I frown, not liking what he is suggesting but fair is fair, his past for mine. A fair trade but I had done so much to forget, to bury and to bring it all back up, the gaping hole I tried to patch, will only burst open.

"All right," I murmur, feeling my eyes getting heavier. "You have a deal."

"Very well, now get some sleep," he whispers softly.

I nod, letting my eyes close, embracing me in the darkness once more.

***

Home is not a place, it's the people inside that makes it a home. All your belongings, antique items, precious furniture mean nothing without the people you share it with. *'Things are replaceable, lives aren't.'* It had stuck with me since last month, clinging onto it, believing I have a place to call home. Even if it is short-lived, I know I can rely on Syrus.

"Could you pass me that nail?" Syrus asks me, snapping from my thoughts. I nod and pass the iron nail, watching Syrus repair the wall of an old shack. Two elderly people lived in it, far away from the small town and still close to the city. (Well, with our speed, it's close.)

Syrus takes a step back, admiring his handy work. Pride struck him as he looks at me with a big smile. It is unnerving. I am so used to the vampire's sullen features, to see him smile, is slightly creepy.

"What?" he stops smiling, concern only then takes its hold. I shrug.

"Nothing looks good," I smile back, and Syrus eases.

Putting the supplies away in another room, he comes back tossing me a pair of boots. I catch them and look down at the black leather shoes, covered in mud. "What's this for?" I ask him, taking holding the boot.

"For you to wear, have to blend in a little," Syrus explains, rummaging through the rooms in the house.

"Why?"

"To go hunting, there's a celebration tonight."

Storytime

Breathing has become a useful habit, undeeded, but usueful. I still breathe the surrounding air, in taking all the scents and smells of the world. I can just picture what is nearby, but smell what is also far away. The smell of burning wood, cooked meats, the spilling ale, the wet mud, mixed with manure and the enticing aroma of human blood. They all swirl and mix as Syrus, and I get ready to leave. I am already eager to tear into the flesh of humans, just to drain their sweet blood from within.

The breeze picks up, shouts and laughter of humans carried by the wind and the sunsets upon the horizon. They play music the people dance together. They keep warm near the bonfire and drink away the night. I give a small smile as I watch them bond together in the moonlight, all happy. I only become envious, as I desire this, not with humans, no, but with my kind, accepted and welcomed with open arms.

"What's the celebration for?" I ask Syrus as we watch from a distance, seeking lone humans to wander away from the crowds.

"For a bountiful season, apparently the harvest was good this year," Syrus explains, his eyes watching the group of drunken men glaring at the crowd. Summer is my favourite season, it's warm, a little too much if you sit in the rays for too long, but it's better than winter. We don't have to worry about snow—snow I hate winter, I hate snow, it was always cold, I was always cold. "Are you all right?" Syrus asks me, snapping me out of my bitter thoughts about snow.

"Yes, I'm okay," I smile at the older vampire. Not convinced, Syrus stares at me a little longer.

"All - right," Syrus clears his throat and pays his attention back to the crowd.

"So what's your story?" I ask Syrus before bursting into laughter at the poor performance the villagers display for tonight's festival.

"My story?" he asks, watching the villagers dance.

"It's been a month, remember, deals a deal," I snicker looking up to the older vampire. Syrus playfully shakes his head at me.

"You pick the oddest times," he sighs and relaxes against the stone wall.

My smile disappears as I watch his face contort. Digging deep into his memory, his smile fades, his eyes sullenly look away from the festivities, facing the muddy ground.

He takes a deep breath, his jaw clenches and unclenched while doing so.

"Y-you don't have to," I timidly add, carefully touching his arm.

He relaxes under my touch and looks at me with sorrow.

"No, it's—okay. I -," Syrus stops himself, searching for the right words. "I haven't spoken to anyone about this," he murmurs.

"You still don't have to tell me," I whisper. An enormous weight feels heavy on my chest, unable to shake the guilt away.

Syrus gives a sweet smile and affectionately ruffles my hair. I huff and bat his hand away, something he started a week ago when I got a math problem right. I hate the gesture, but it eases the ache inside. Deep down, I didn't really mind it.

"For most of my human life, others hated and feared me," he begins, looking back to the partying villagers. "Growing up, I got used to it. During that time, I fell in love. She was my light, my life, my everything. She had so much faith in me, not once did she see a monster, she saw a boy who needed a friend, and then a man who she can love," Syrus's voice cracked, he clears it and continues. "But everything came crashing down again when I lost her," Syrus murmurs, watching the fire dance, the bright orange of the flames reflecting off his eyes. "My everything, my love—they took her away from me." A small tear escapes from his dark grey eyes.

"Why?" I ask my voice, barely a whisper.

"Hatred, my entire existence is the reason for her death," he answers simply. "And I was powerless," he adds and then looking back at me. "I would happily have waited for death, but of course fate had other plans," he finishes.

Vampirism.

"I'm –."

"Don't be, you didn't kill her, you weren't even born then," he interrupts me. I nod slowly, keeping my mouth shut.

"Would you end your own existence?" I ask, swallowing the lump in my throat.

"I - I see this as some justified punishment for myself. I became the monster she denied me to be, and if I die at the hands of a hunter, then I would accept it. But for now, I just wonder the earth, uninterested in life, hoping a hunter will come by."

Hunters swarm every nook and cranny of this earth. Heck, there are more hunters than there are vampires. Our species is going extinct, that is no lie, so I am surprised no hunter has taken this advantage. A vampire who wishes to die, who barely eats. Any hunter would have taken the chance.

"And now there's me," I confirm with him. Syrus cracks a small smile.

"And I don't regret it," Syrus quickly puts in. I felt my heart starting up again as I heard those words. Staring up at him in awe. "I will always yearn for death, but I still want a family, that much is true and as time goes by, I'm starting hate myself a little less," Syrus whispers, his smile going away, going back deep into his thoughts.

"So are there others you have turned?" I clarify, and Syrus shakes his head and looks back at me.

"No, you are the only one." He answers, giving me a warm smile. "The last five hundred years, I have only wallowed in self-pity, mourning over my love. I did not care to turn another, let alone care for other vampires," he explains a little more.

I feel my heartbreak a little, letting doubt seep into the cracks, hopelessness soon followed. Syrus seems to notice the pain deep inside me. He takes an unneeded breath and looks back at the villagers.

"Now, since I've bared my soul, are you hungry?" he asks me, swiftly changing the topic.

I swallow the large lump in my throat, quickly replaced with the sharp burning. I nod, looking over to the festivities. The mix of fire and the human scent wafts heavily in the air. I feel my incisors ache. Passing every face, looking over every detail, ignoring gender, I searched until I found what I wanted. I take one step forward, a growl resonates from my chest. *Mine.* Syrus quickly grabs onto my shirt and pulling me back. I hiss at the older vampire. Infuriated that he stopped me from getting to my meal. "You need to be more aware of your surroundings," Syrus coos, lifting my head ever so slightly. A man, armed to the teeth, observing my prey dance. *A father? Brother? An ordinary hunter? This is only a minor setback.*

"I want her," I murmur.

"I know, but its time you learned self-control," Syrus puts in. I snarl in disagreement. "Patience, little one. Allow me to distract this hunter just so you can get close but do not attack. Understood?" Syrus asks me. I barely register his words, I am too engrossed with the girl's scent, the way her heart pulses, life-giving blood, beneath her skin. I want to tear it apart and feast. *It will feel so good, life pouring into my veins, its desperate cries, all but sweet music, satisfying the cruel beast.* "Rune!" Syrus snaps. I look at him, the trance breaking. I slightly cower in fear, wondering what I have done wrong. Syrus gives a heavy sigh. "Do you understand?" he asks again, and I think back.

Distract hunter, get close, don't attack and—and.

"What do I do when I get close?" I ask innocently. Uncertainty fills my insides, becoming on edge. *I only had Syrus lure my meals and let me attack.*

"You lure her away, find a safe place and eat," he explains as if it is simple. I take a step back and slightly cower behind Syrus. I felt unease. My head fills with thoughts stringing together doubt and fear. *What if I can't do this? What if he finds me, what if he kills me.* "I won't let anything happen to you," Syrus reassures me as if he could read my thoughts.

Syrus has explained a newborns mentality is the same as a toddler, all we want to do is eat and sleep for the first six months, self-control is near impossible at the first three, but is crucial to learn before the six-month mark. Our mentality returns to the age before we became a vampire. It's a degrading thought, but it makes sense. I was more cocky, brave even. I wouldn't turn this challenge away. But now, I want Syrus to take care of everything. I don't want to do this on my own.

"You'll be fine," he assures, putting his hand on my head, gently patting my head. I take comfort in the slight gesture and nod slowly.

"Promise," I whisper and Syrus promises.

Syrus becomes an entirely di fferent person, walking to the group as some drunkard and cheers with the men, becoming obnoxious to any barmaid and woman passing by. It's incredible to watch, a whole different persona comes to life. Where did this alternative personality come from?

This catches hunter's attention, unhappy with the developing situation. All the young men become more rowdy and demanding, grating on the hunter's nerve even more. Moving away from his post, I make my move. Ignoring the sweet smell wafting in the air, the sound of pumping blood through every heartbeat. I struggle to keep things under control. I want to act, give in, bare my teeth and kill. But there she is, dancing so happily, so freely, the urge only grows deeper, wanting to tear the innocent life away. She notices me coming closer, smiling. She moves to me, closing the gap.

"I have never seen you before," she coos. "Just arrived in town?" she asks flirtatiously. *You're making this too easy.*

"Just arrived," I answer, dancing to the music alongside her. The urge to kill dwindles as another grows. One that wants to play, one that wants to cause suffering, all to make the kill sweeter.

"By yourself?" she questions, her suspicions grew. I chuckle, trying to ease her nerves.

"Of course not, I am here with my fa-." I stop myself mid-sentence. I look back to Syrus. Watching him cheer and dance with the other humans, and starting a fight with the girl's father. "I'm here with a friend," I correct myself. My insides twist, my mouth bitter as I say that word. *Friend. What was I thinking?*

"Well, since my father is busy, with your—'friend' do you want to go somewhere private?" she asks coy. Her smile says it all. *Naughty. Certainly rebellious. It's a pity that it will get you killed.*

"Certainly," I reply delicately grasping her hand and letting her lead us away from the party.

Heading around a wooden house, away from the flames lights, covered by the shadows and our mouths already connected. The human is, unfortunately, too eager. I take control and pin her to the wall, my mouth trailing kisses to her neck. My tongue tracing the central artery, the heat from her skin ignites the hunger, reminding me why I am here. I waste no more time and viciously bit into the skin. She screams, but I swiftly cover her mouth, drinking every mouthful. *So warm.* Taking my time as I savour the taste, sweet but a little tangy.

Letting go of the body, enjoying pleasure coursing through my veins, dousing the burning fire deep within. *So good.* I lick all the blood around my mouth, desperate for more. I focus my hearing, all those beating hearts, the crackling fire, the cheering and the music. Slowly I become calm, able to restrain myself. Staring at the lifeless body before my feet, noting her perfect skin, dark hair, pretty green eyes. She was very alluring. *Pity, she would have been a good vampire.*

'she is not one of us.' A whisper in my subconscious tells me. I frown, not understanding what it means, but I trust it. A wave of drowsiness washes over me, already searching for a place to rest my head.

"That didn't take long," Recognising the presence, I nod in agreement and shuffle to the person, dragging my heavy feet along.

"I'm tired," I murmur. I look up to Syrus, a bewildered expression on his face.

"You don't want to join the party?" he asks me, and I shake my head. *Stupid newborn body, stupid newborn mentality.* Syrus smiles in understanding and ruffles my hair. I still hate it, but I allow it just this once. "Let's get you home," he insists, and I nod. Closely following the vampire behind. The noise of the party got softer and softer as we walk away from the town. All we have is the silence of the fields and cries from the animals of the night. "I'm proud of you," Syrus pipes up, just a few minutes before we arrive home. I looked at the vampire, tired and confused

I couldn't put two and two together. "It terrified you to control yourself, let alone go up to the girl. You did well. I'm proud," Syrus explains further. Apart from me wanted to cry right there and then. So many emotions mix, becoming impossible to pinpoint exactly which one. My throat becomes tights, and my chest heavy.

What is this feeling?

Syrus seems to notice but says nothing and leads me inside, carefully guiding me to my room. I'm too tired to change, let alone care about my blood-stained clothes, I walk over to my bed and collapse on top, allowing the darkness succumb to me.

"What's so special about magic father?" I asked him as he gazes at my mother's portrait. It had only been a month, and my father still mourns for her. He turns to me with a smile, gently walking over, and scoops me into his arms.

"Magic, is what makes this family," he begins. "For generations, we have mystical abilities above average humans," he snaps his fingers and the curtains close and the candles lit by themselves. "And our family is a respected member of our society," he prides, as the coat of arms illuminates over the mantle of the fireplace. Two trees, one upright, the other upside down, their roots entwining together. "You will be a great warlock, just like me, and your father's before you."

Yer a Vampire, Rune

It's been a week since I first hunted by myself. It has been a change, seeking a meal in the open streets, always watching my back. Even if Syrus is close by, I am still on edge. Too many terrible memories of hunters pinning me down at my most vulnerable and nearly slicing my head off. If we are the most potent species, how are we so quickly taken down? It's so frustrating. Thinking back, I realise how easy it was for me to fixate on human blood. The need to drink, to quench this cruel thirst. The world around becomes irrelevant. An easy target for hunters. But now, I am a little more aware, able to pull away when the enemy strikes.

I wonder if Syrus is eating, there are more humans in this city, breaking in, feeding, and getting out would be easy for him.

I notice a small dull light around the corner of an old stone building. Illuminating the little side street. Only one heartbeat, luring me closer to the lone prey. A growl resonates from my throat, eager to pounce on the lone human, sinking my teeth into their flesh.

Jumping around the corner, claws out, fangs bared, but there was no one, even the small light is gone. I am once again shrouded in darkness. I frown, walking deeper into the street, searching around my surroundings.

"So the hunter was telling the truth," a sassy voice coos in the dark.

I turn to see no one behind me, nothing.

"Where are you?" I growl, baring my fangs, showing off my clawed hands, hoping to scare the enemy.

"A vampire," the voice scoffs, tsking at me at the same time. "Your father will not be happy about this." I freeze. The memories I have buried for so long have bubbled up to the surface. The need for air has never been more crucial. My mind frantically jumps from one thought to another. I cannot calm myself. The darkness laughs at me, surrounding me once more, swallowing me whole. *Please make it stop.* "Oh well, I'll get rid of you myself," a fiery glow sparks in the shadows, a menacing smile behind it. *Warlock.* I'm stuck in place, watching the fireball fly towards me. I embrace the fiery burn to embrace my skin. The fire comes closer, feeling the warmth radiate from it, but it never became my demise.

Syrus stands tall in between me, and the fiery blaze coming toward us. *No, please!* I watch Syrus engulfed in flames, coiling around him like a fiery serpent. In disbelief, the fire didn't singe Syrus's skin, they slowly dissipate into thin air. The warlocks mouth drops, he trembles, and Syrus takes another step closer.

"Wh-who are you?" the warlock stutters, ready to run in the other direction. Syrus didn't answer him, taking another step forward. The air becomes still, oppressive even. Chills run down my spine, watching the other vampire. *Something is coming.*

A shadowed claw comes from the ground, pulling itself from the shadows itself. I fall back on to my bottom, watching in horror as the inky humanoid shape, with long spindly arms, its hands dragging across the ground as it slowly walks to the enemy, many of them different shapes and sizes, coming from the walls, the ground, stopping the warlock in his trackzs. They pounce upon the warlock. He screeches as many of these shadowed creatures clamours over him.

"Please, please!" he cries. "I'll do anything." He begs some more. Syrus steps closer to the warlock, stilling as the older vampire approaches. The shadowed creatures almost succumb to his body, face and outstretched arm are all but left as the rest covered in shadows. I hesitantly get up and move closer, wanting to get a better look at the warlocks expression. Fear, absolute fear resonating off in waves.

"Care to explain why you wish to kill my child," Syrus asks cooly. Flashing his fangs.

Child?

"I was just doing what I was told!" he cries, trying to get out the shadow's grip. Syrus snarls at him and grabs his hair by the handful. He winces, tears form. "The boy's father, he ordered this, he wanted the boy dead!" he screams, followed by uncontrollable sobbing. My stomach drops. My body shakes, memories take over my mind. I grip the sides of my head as they all pool into the forefront of my mind, remembering the rituals, the spells, the potions, all-because—because.

"I couldn't use magic," I murmur. Tears spring to my eyes, falling onto the stone ground. "All because I couldn't use magic," I curl myself into a little ball. Unable to stop shaking. "It made little sense," I whine, "None of it did," I whisper to myself. "I tried to be a dutiful son. I did everything he has asked of me. I study every night till I collapsed, I partook in every ritual, I dealt with the pain he inflicted, I drank every potion, I tried so hard to use magic. So hard, but I couldn't. I couldn't use it." I cry to myself.

Curling into myself even more. "I just wanted him to accept me. I just wanted us to be a family."

"Do what you want with him," I hear Syrus rumble and screams erupt. Squelching sounds heard within the little street, bones snapping in two, the flesh torn apart, blood splattering onto the ground, screams drowned out by gurgling and then finally dull to silence.

I felt a pair of powerful arms wrap around me, pulling me onto their lap and hold me tight. I welcomed the embrace and held on tightly.

"It's going to be ok," Syrus murmurs. I heave into his chest, letting out the bottled emotions that I have hidden away for so long.

"I tried, I tried, I tried," I mutter repeatedly, the tears not stopping. Syrus just holds me, letting me cry it all out. "I was never good enough, nothing I did was good enough," I mumble into Syrus's chest. "Kicking me out when there was nothing he could do, disowning me as his son," I weep, shaking in Syrus's arms. "I did everything I could to make him proud." Syrus remained silent as he held me tight, listening to my mutterings repeatedly. It was like a wound finally breaking open, for not healing so long, bleeding and pouring out to any poor soul who had witnessed the burst. "Why did it matter?" I murmur. "Why did it matter if I could use magic? Isn't a parent meant to love their child unconditionally?" asking the world, not caring if Syrus answered or not. I always wanted to know, know why it mattered to him so much. I cling onto Syrus's shirt, staining it with tears, and now soaking wet.

"Not all parents are like that, unfortunately," Syrus whispers. "Some are so consumed with their image, passing the torch of the family name. I have seen so many human daughters cast away because they are born first. Mother's treated like slaves because they stay, expected too, giving up all ambitions and dreams of their own, boys called soft and pathetic because they cry because they show genuine emotion, have to be tough and not seen weak. This world is so fucked up because of society's pressures, we become so consumed by them, we forget the essential things in life," Syrus soothes. "I don't envy humans."

"Why, why does it have to be me?" I cry.

"I don't know, the universe has a funny way of planning things, regardless if you like it or not. I should know," Syrus humour as if he is in some hidden joke. "But I will say one thing," Syrus continues, holding me close. "If I ever meet that bastard, I will destroy him," he says calmly, his voice deepening as if had also swallowed gravel. Fear would initially kick in. The dense atmosphere returned, but only for a quick second before going back to normal.

"Syrus," I croak. He hums, still holding me. "What are you?"

"A Vampire . . . but not an ordinary one. I didn't exactly tell you why I'm hated," he chuckles gently. "Like you, I asked the universe why, I fought it and disagreed with it. But my fate had already being sealed, no matter who fought on my behalf, everyone in Rome was right, I was to be a monster." He explains vaguely. "King—heh, I hate that title. Five hundred years and it's bitter on my tongue. How can I call myself a king when I have no interest in saving our species."

"I've read about you," I sniffle into his chest. "His grimoires spoke of a vampire with abilities like no other. Born and turned at twenty-one, without turning by another vampire's bite."

"Looks like I don't have to explain the rest," Syrus muses, I huff out a laugh, feeling calmer in the vampire's arms, distracting myself from the past, but an ache is still there, a fear crawling up my spine, lingering in the back of my head, cruelly reminding me of what is coming in three months.

"Syrus," I spoke his name again. "Please don't leave," I whisper, tears leaking from my eyes.

"What gave you that idea?" he asks me, gently patting my head.

"You said that once I can look after myself, you would leave and hating life and die," I whimper.

"I'm not going anywhere. I will always crave death as I wish to see her once again, I've lasted five hundred years attempting to end it all and just like I said, the universe has a funny way of planning things, regardless if you like it or not," I ease at his words. Relaxing once more into his arms, feeling sleepy once more.

"Promise?" I respond tiredly, letting my eyes close.

"Promise."

What it means to be king

Syrus and I had gone for a stroll through the bright green fields before winter arrives and settles the countryside in snow. Enjoying the lasts moments of summer before dreaded old man winter comes knocking in. *I hate winter.* It's unexpected but pleasant, something a human would struggle to wrap their minds around, a monster, a vampire waltzing through the fields, enjoying nature—my that's a human thing, vampires prefer to lurk in dark caves and hide under children's beds and scare them for fun. Not that I want too, but scaring little humans can be fun. We still maintain those human qualities, but just like humans, we show care and affection for our species, and not for our food.

"Do you know this flower?" Syrus asks me as he trudges through the tall grass. I look at the flower in his hand, white petals and a yellow centre. I frown at the plant in his hand—I never really cared much for flowers.

"Ah, a white flower," I answer and Syrus just laughs, shaking his head.

"You are right; it is a white flower, but it's also known as chamomile. It has healing properties, apothecaries use this for medicines," Syrus explains and opening the book that is in his other hand and puts the flower in and closing it once more.

"Why are you telling me this? We just heal from our injures immediately," I explain, curious why he put the flower in the book.

"It doesn't hurt to learn about medicine. I rather know things, then remain ignorant," Syrus explains, walking through the tall grass.

"Ok, so why put it in the book?" I ask, sating my curiosity as I follow him.

"When you press flowers and herbs in books or paper, they preserve and last longer. They don't wilt. I don't exactly know why, but one day, I'm sure we will figure it out," Syrus smiles, looking at the closed book.

I shrug, satisfied with the answer.

"So, you have a last name or something?" I ask, making small talk. Syrus raises an eyebrow looking at me.

"Why do you ask?" Syrus answers my question with his question.

"Well . . . I had one . . . but not anymore," I shrug, not really having a reason to know Syrus's last name. Syrus stares at me for a while before breaking.

"Valerius," he answers in a mumble, turning his bead down to the grass and moving his feet forward.

"Huh, interesting. Is that Greek?" I ask, and Syrus shrugs.

"Roman, not that it matters, it's just a name, it holds nothing," Syrus murmurs.

"Makes sense, since you are just over five hundred years," I respond, shrugging my shoulders afterwards. I look up ahead and see a hill, smiling I tap Syrus's arm, gaining his attention. "Race ya to the top," I point to the slope, thus achieving a grin from the older vampire.

Syrus and I stop, counting down from three, and launch ourselves towards the hill. The wind blowing through my hair, my body not desperate for air or getting tired, I felt like I could get farther than the hill, past the city, anywhere with the speed I am going at.

Syrus smiles as he waits for me at the top, my jaw drops as I see him standing there. I look back to the levelled plane we were standing on and then back to Syrus.

"How did you?" I stop myself waiting for the older vampire to answer.

"I'm older, therefore, faster than you," he gloats, rubbing my head, messing up my hair again. I sigh and flatten the mess he made and fall to the ground, and lying on the short grass, enjoying the sun's warmth.

"Break time," I smile, closing my eyes and covering them with my arm, so my vision is in complete darkness.

"We've been walking for fifteen minutes," Syrus chuckles, and I shrug my shoulders in response.

"So . . ." I let it drawl out. "What are those black shadow people—creature things?" I ask as I jumble my words, waving my spare hand in the air. I hear Syrus sit down next to me, resounding with a sigh afterwards.

"Souls that I have devoured over the centuries," he huffs. "Whenever I feed and drain the life from their bodies, their soul becomes subservient to me. Though sometimes they don't listen to me," Syrus growls.

"Like what?" I ask, removing my arm and looking over to the older vampire, I can barely open my eyes without being blinded by the sun.

"They ignore my wishes when I don't want to eat," he huffs. "Or defend me when I am about to end up dead, it is rather frustrating," Syrus glares at his own shadow. "But other than that, they are useful when I want things to get done quicker or learning information. I can block their constant nattering out and only listen to the ones who are brave enough to speak with me directly," he explains, leaning back and basking in the sun.

"How does that work?"

"They talk into my ear, the others hide in the shadows, always talking, always speaking to each other and not to me. It was irritating, maddening even as time went on. It took me a while to block it out, finally silence."

"Huh . . . do you have any other abilities?" I ask, moving forward from the shadows, Syrus only shrugs.

"Unable to burn in fire is one and walking through shadows," is all he replies, putting the book over his face, to shield him from the sun. I knew I should have brought a book along.

"What? Walkthrough shadows? How does that work?" I sit up in surprise, Syrus shrugs once more.

"I don't know, it just happens - I can enter a home without opening a door or window, ambling to get into places that others could not. Wherever there is a shadow I can hide and walk into it," he explains. I felt a slight uneasiness in the pit of my stomach.

"Was that you in while I was bathing?" I ask, feeling rage burn within my chest. Syrus lifts the book from his face, frowning.

"No - I think you can guess who it really was," he grumbles, putting the book back on his.

"It was the shadows you control," I mumble and laid back on the grass.

"Yep, remember when I told you they do things of their own free will," Syrus reminds me.

"Unfortunately, yes." I sigh. "Any other abilities you have?"

"Nothing. I'm sure I will learn as time goes along—if I ever live that long," Syrus mutters, flailing his own hand. I tsk at the vampire and close my own eyes again, just enjoying the warm sensation on my skin as the sunbeams down. It's pleasant, even if it affects me a little.

"It's weird to think you are the king, though. I expected you to be . . ."

"Taller?" I burst out into laughter.

"No," I laugh, trying to calm myself down. "Like more bloodthirsty or power-hungry, not . . . quick-witted and composed," I explain.

"Many expect that I know little about the previous heirs, but from what I have experienced, many fear who I am, and it's not just because I am a vampire but what I am capable of," I hum in thought mulling over his words.

"But you have done nothing," I reply.

"I brought Rome to its knees, but that was a long time ago," Syrus clarifies.

"Ah, that would cause any alarm for concern," I giggle. "But what about your people, do they know you're here?"

"Some do, but only a handful. They follow me from city to city, hoping I would take on my role. They are irritating," Syrus deadpans. I remove my arm and sit up, letting my eyes slowly adjust to the brightness again, blinking the tears away before looking over to Syrus. Still lying down with a book on his face.

"Do you still want too?" I ask him, and he shrugs.

"Maybe, I have considered it lately, but I know I am not ready yet," he sighs, sounding more gravely in his voice. I look to the horizon, watching the tall grass dance in the wind, the leaves shake and the wind whistles as it flies across the countryside.

"I think you would be a good King," I say out loud, but I am given no response.

The vampire lays dormant, unnerving considering his chest doesn't rise and fall. Scooting closer, I gently lift the book. His eyes are closed, unflinching to the sun's rays. I smile and lightly put the book back down. I rarely see him sleep. Syrus explained to me he can go days without shutting an eye, I envy him as I wish to sleep less, able to stay up as long as Syrus can, just reading or hunting, something more entertaining.

Turned by the king of vampire's himself, I wonder if I have any special abilities, or am I just normal like the rest of them—you know what, I don't mind, I'm happy to be an average vampire, as long as I am with Syrus, I don't care.

Note to self, lock doors

Syrus and I raced back to the wooden cabin, I am at a disadvantage considering I am still new, but I am determined to win this time. Spending a month here has helped me memorise the area—I know a shortcut or two. Syrus played fair and not ask of his shadow minions to help him achieve success. We drew closer to the finishing line, and we both began using all kinds of methods to trip each other up just so one can assure victory. Getting closer and closer to the door my desire to win overtook me and in the last attempt, tackle Syrus to the ground, we wrestle to get to the door, holding each other down. As much as we tried to be serious about this, we couldn't help but burst into laughter, as we push each other away, to win, but this is all cut short as Syrus puts me into a headlock.

"C'mon that's cheating!" I laugh, trying to wrestle out of his iron grip hold.

"Last I checked, this was still within the rules," Syrus teases as he pulls me along and grabs the doorknob.

"Says the guy ten times stronger than me," I laugh.

"You did well to hold me off," Syrus rebuts with a laugh.

"Yeah, but it would be a different story if I was older," I grunt, still holding a smile on my face. Syrus laughs it off and opens the door, finally letting me go, but not without repercussions to his actions and pin him to the floor. Try as I might, I could not hold him down for long and once more I am in a headlock.

"Ok, ok, I yield," I laugh, but Syrus doesn't let go.

"I don't know, it could be another trap," he responds teasingly.

"No, It's not a trap, I promise," I laugh "I promise." Syrus lets go, and I continue to laugh at the situation. My belly hurt so much from laughing, but I only stop when I notice two things. One; Syrus stopped laughing abruptly and two; the deadly look he gave in the distance. My eyes wander over to the darkness, a figure standing tall before us, watching in disgust.

"Well, that certainly was a warming site," the man murmurs, stepping out from the dark. My heart plummeted into my stomach, eyes growing wide as dinner plates. My body trembles as if I am in the middle of winter, unable to keep warm in the cold. I slowly crawl backwards, desperately trying to keep my distance as he draws closer. Tears threatening to escape as I desperately pretend the man who experimented on me, the man who cast me aside, the man who denounced me as his son, is not here, he's not real. "A vampire, how . . . disappointing," he glowers. I instinctively bow my head, remembering this feeling, the shame brought down upon my head, disappointing a parental figure. Syrus gets up from the ground, stopping my father in his place, standing in front of me, shielding me from him. "Ah yes, I have you to thank, don't I?" he smirks, and with a flick of a wrist, he flings Syrus to another side of the house. "Your kind is dangerous that I will admit but useless against an experienced warlock," father looms over me. "Therefore, you, should have been a warlock," he sneers, his hollow black eyes stare into mine.

"Yet you cast him out," Syrus snarls, his claws growing, fangs bared at the warlock. "All because he couldn't use magic, why go to so much effort?" Syrus hisses, rage burning deep within his eyes, ready to draw blood at any second. My father sighs, taking out a vial full of red liquid from his pocket. My eyes widened, recognising the spell he is about to use. To bend the laws of nature, transporting whoever he desires away, the same spell he used to cast me out.

"No," I scream out, standing in Syrus's way. "I won't let you do this," my voice cracks as tears continue to spill. "I'm not going anywhere, nor is Syrus, I chose this, and I'm happy—for once in my goddamn life. I am happy, please . . . if you really care –. . . just leave us alone," I beg. My father sighs. Rage burns up within him, shooting daggers at Syrus, glaring at the vampire with pure hatred.

"You don't have a choice. Our Family demands it, our name respected amongst the magical community, only turned into a laughingstock. A boy who cannot use magic, and now turned into a leech, and as head of this family, I must destroy this shame." Syrus pushes past me, lunging for the warlock. Fury had taken over his senses. The warlock chants, and blood comes out from the vial, forcing a door to open before swiftly moving out of the way and Syrus falling through and shutting before he can get back up.

"Where . . . where did you send him?" I quiver.

"Somewhere, where he can't escape," he replies and swiftly grabs my arm, chanting another verse and summon another door before pulling me through.

I land on my hands and knees, still shaken by the events unfolding. Tears haven't been able to stop since his arrival. I feel so weak, so useless, not once did I fight back,

I could have fought back, but . . . I didn't. Syrus he's gone, and I'm alone.

The warlock snaps his fingers and the sounds of chains clattering and clanking slithering against the floor, and the two cuffs snap at my wrists like vipers, chaining to the brick wall and pulling me closer. I tug and fight, but to avail, I am strung up against the wall. I watch him slice his own finger, my own senses crave for the blood, wanting it as I watch him draw a pentagram on the floor, chanting as he goes along. *A trap?*

I look around the square room, recognising the stone walls, the scent of burning lavender, the distant sounds of bubbling and boiling water. My old home . . . I never thought I would end up here.

Sand, sand everywhere

Syrus falls. Falling from the portal he foolishly fell from. Syrus could only throw curses at himself as he plummets to the sea of sand below. The harsh sun blaring down upon him, the hot winds rise as he falls below. Syrus braces himself and hits the sand. Bones break and snap, his vision blurs and blackens, pain erupts and fires through his nerves. Syrus felt winded, though he didn't need the air, he felt all the air in his body escape him when hitting the ground. For Syrus, this isn't the first time he has fallen from tall structures.

The bastard truly believes Syrus is just an ordinary vampire, throwing him away to a destitute land where no human or animal found for miles. An ordinary vampire would perish from starvation before finding civilisation again, drying up and becoming a living husk. Vampires cannot die from starvation, only go mad with hunger and falling into a deep slumber where their dreams filled with the hunt.

The shadow to cast right now is Syrus's, the sand dunes cannot cast a shadow, the harsh sunlight burns down above. Syrus loathed himself for scorning his actions, to be reckless and easily defeated, thrown out so quickly and put in a position where he has to wait for nightfall before he can do anything. He failed Rune, the vampire he promised to protect, Rune's waiting for him, pleading for Syrus to save him. A growl rises from Syrus's throat, pushing his body to heal faster, ignoring the searing pain with each limb and digit Syrus moves. Hobbling to get onto his hands and knees, Syrus breathes through the pain, feeling bones pop and creak, some going back into place, others protruding from the skin.

"Where is he?" he asks the shadows, hiding within Syrus's shadow for safety. Wherever there is darkness in the world, they can traverse through and seek the answers Syrus requires.

'A castle . . . far away . . . cold . . . winds filled with snow . . . we can show you the way.' One whispers in his ear. Syrus looks up to the pristine blue sky. Not until nightfall. The magical community has its magic to move from one place to another, and Syrus has his. Once the sun sets, Syrus can use his powers to walk through the darkness, ambling him to go anywhere he pleases.

***

I remained chained to the wall for the last day, the night finally arriving once more, and I am feeling a little hopeless. What if Syrus disappeared, what if he cannot find his way back, what if he lost in some land unable to be free? No. Syrus is different, he's no ordinary vampire if anyone can get out of it, he can.

The doors to my cell creak open, the warlock waltzing in, and a floating mirror slowly follows behind him. The wooden doors close with a loud thunk, echoing within the large empty room.

"I came across an interesting image," he announces to me, the mirror coming closer to me. My eyes widen at the projected image, Syrus in the halls, claws out, teeth bared, calling for my name.

"Impressive, that he found us and he got back here so quickly." the warlock sighs, moving the mirror away, his eyes boring down into the mine. "Now how did he do that?" he glowers and brings forth the knife from his pocket once more.

"I'm not telling you," I hiss, gaining some courage.

"Oh, you will cause if you don't, I'll kill him first," he smirks, drawing the blade closer to my neck.

"How about I show you?" Syrus asks cooly, the door smashed to pieces, his glowing fiery red eyes burn as he stalks towards us.

"Syrus, watch o-." the warlock slashed me across the face with his blade, Syrus appears before him, throwing him against the wall. Hearing a satisfying crack and turns to me, inspecting my wound.

"Are you all right?" he asks, gently cupping my cheek, relieved to see my healing has kicked in. I nodded, feeling my flesh stitch back together, the blood flowing from my mouth, coming to a stop.

"Die!" the warlock yells, summoning a ball of fire but Syrus can take on the heat and leap towards the warlock pinning him to the ground, his clawed hand slashing against his skin, he screeches in agony and thrusts Syrus back onto the pentagram. *No!*

Black smog surrounds Syrus as he gets up, succumbing to the vampire in a transcendent sleep. He stills, his eyes going white and no longer can he respond to my cries.

The Warlock gets up, his face bleeding like a waterfall, his nose just hanging by a piece of flesh. Growling, he sticks his nose back on and begins chanting his spell. Healing all the wounds on his face, as if it never happened.

Syrus, please snap out of this!

A Promise

"There you are!" Annabeth exclaims, coming out from Syrus's little house. A bright, toothy smile greets him as his eyes lands on her. Surprised, not shocked to see her standing there, alive, beautiful, as if she had never died. Syrus's eyes popped from his head, staring at her like a goldfish out of water. Annabeth frowns slightly, confused why her husband looks at her like this. She grabs onto his hands, bringing him closer to her, and she studies his shocked expression. Syrus took notice of the bump in her stomach, poking out, just touching his own.

"You're pregnant?" he asks her, bewildered. Her frown deepens.

"Of course, I am. Are you all right, did you hit your head?" she asks, putting both of her hands on either side of his cheeks. Syrus nods, tears flowing down his face as he gently grabs her hand. To touch it once more, to feel her warmth. His heart only ached to be with her, to love her.

"I just thought I never see you again," Annabeth, obviously confused but smiles sweetly at the vampire.

"I'm here, and so is our child. We are both here," She soothes, bringing her lips to his. Syrus welcomed the kiss, the feeling of her soft lips against his.

His best friend, his love, his life, right before him.

"I've missed you," Syrus says, kissing his love once again.

"I've missed you," she responds in between kisses and then grabbing his hand. "Now come," she says, pulling his hand eagerly. "Alexandros is waiting for us," she earnestly states, pulling him into the house.

Alexandros get up from his seat, his eyes have more wrinkles than Syrus last remembered, his hair had greyed, thinned even. He eagerly greets Syrus with a hug, patting him on the back.

"Ah—together, at last, my son, my daughter, and soon to be grandson," Alexandros laughs merrily. Annabeth could only roll her eyes and sit down, holding her belly.

"He could be a girl, don't get your hopes up, just yet," she tuts. Alexandros waves his hand and looks to Syrus.

"What do you think, boy? We'll have a healthy son or girl?" he chuckles, egging Annabeth on.

Syrus just stood between them, dumbfounded that this conversation is happening. None of it could be real, could it? Everything he ever wanted is right here before him, a family, a place to call home. Syrus looks to Annabeth, in awe of the bulging belly, his heart leaping with joy, pride, excitement. He would love them, cherish them, no matter the gender, he would teach them everything he knew and so forth. He wouldn't care as long as they were happy, healthy and everyone is together. A family, Syrus always wanted a family.

Rune . . .The thought of the young vampire, the vampire Syrus turned with his own blood, the vampire he taught, the vampire he let into his home, shared his belongings, share his story. The boy who cried into his arms as grief had gripped Rune by the throat.

"This isn't real," is all Syrus replies with. Alexandros frowns, and Annabeth remains neutral. "There's a vampire who needs me, a boy, alone and scared

that he would end up that way again. I can't abandon him, I can't leave him, not yet. As much as I want to stay and live out this fantasy, but I just can't. My son . . . my family, is waiting for me."

The world around Syrus turns to smoke, leaving him in pitch darkness. Annabeth stood before him, smiling as she came up to him and cups his face.

"I am so proud of you," she whispers and their foreheads touch. "I never had the chance to tell you to keep living."

"Even if you knew I would be in agony," Syrus sniffles, tears streaking down his face.

"Yes. You are the king, and they need you, my love," she whispers and kisses the top of his forehead. "To me, you were never a monster, vampire or human, you were my best friend and my love." A sob wracks through Syrus, hearing those words stab into the gaping hole of his heart.

"Will you leave?" he croaks, holding her close, fearing she would turn into smoke if he let go.

"I'll be here. I'm always watching, and I will wait till your time has come, to see you again," whispers Annabeth. "Till then look after your son and keep living. Promise?" Syrus sniffles out a laugh and nods.

"I promise, but I can't guarantee if it lasts," he muses. His tears are like a running waterfall by now.

"I know," she smiles, rubbing her thumb against his cheek, wiping the stray tears away, "I love you, Syrus."

"I love you, Annabeth." Her touch wisps away into the darkness and a bright light shine from the depths, bringing Syrus back from the spell they put him under.

Revelation

"That was easier than I thought," he laughs at Syrus, the markings on the floor glowing red. Syrus's eyes glazed over with a white film, his jaw slacked, and his body relaxed, shoulder slumped forward.

"What did you do to him!" I scream at the warlock. He laughs and strides over to Syrus's slumped body, touching Syrus's cheek, observing the vampire's expression.

"Our connection to Mother Nature is essential for any magical member in the community. Although she doesn't speak, and we can never, honestly communicate with her with natural magic. Decay magic is more potent if we wish to get help from her or, the souls that return to her. Awakening them from a slumber within Mother Nature to communicate with them. Aiding us to speak to Mother Nature and to the dead once more but not all awaken to the call," he rambles on, removing his hand from Syrus's face and turning to me. "Right now he would either be experiencing his worst nightmare or a blissful dream, and it all depends who answers the call." Dread pools deep into my stomach, my heart wrenching and breaking in two. I know Syrus well enough to believe he would stay, so much self-hate, so much grief, he would remain in fantasy than face reality.

"Syrus! please snap out of it!" I scream to the unresponsive vampire. He just stares blankly. Not responding to any of my cries, I desperately pull against the chains screeching out in the room. "Please . . . don't leave me," I wallow, falling to the ground and letting the sobs wrack through my body. Begging some divine, some spirit to bring him out from this spell.

"Look at you, how weak you've become," I hear the man who I once called my father, tutting at me, shaking his head in disapproval. "A common leech, you were born better."

"Says the man who kicked me out!" I snarl at him, tears continue to stream down my face. "All because I couldn't use magic!" I roar at him. "Born better? You're the one who cast me out, threw me away. If anyone is to blame, it's you," I hiss, baring my canines at him, as a fiery rage burns within my veins.

He sighs and clicks his fingers. A spark ignites and flames wrapped around me, burning my skin. I clench my jaw, refusing to give in. Not once will I give him the satisfaction. The flames die down, and no longer singe my skin, I can feel it heal and stitch itself back together. The pain slowly subsides, and my hunger ignites.

"I did this for you, pushing your limits, and the magic would awaken within you," he clarifies, sounding more sincere.

"Liar," I rasp. "You knew I would never get magic, you just couldn't live knowing that," I cough.

He kicks me in the ribs, sending me back and hitting the brick wall. The chains clatter against the floor, my vision blurs as the back of my skull throbs.

"And no son of mine will exist as a disgusting leech," he glowers, manifesting a sword out of thin air.

"I'm not your son," I growled, our eyes locking onto one another, a standoff between wills, both not willing to look away or blink. He huffs and raises his weapon, ready to swing, his arm throwing down, but stopped as a shadowed hand grabs his wrist. He stood there in shock, unresponsive to the blackface he stares at, and then thrown across the room. I look to Syrus, hoping he had broking through the spell, but my heart only sunk as he stares absentmindedly into the air.

"You're helping me—why?" the shadow doesn't respond, but stands in front of me, guarding me, silently watching the warlock get from the ground.

"So, no ordinary vampire turned you. It explains how he got out the first time," he growls, placing the sword across the Syrus's neck and the shadows around react, quickly attacking the warlock protecting their master. He smiles, chanting a spell, and bright lights emit from his hand, disintegrating the enraged shadows. "So the king has returned," he laughs, pushing the motionless vampire down to the ground. "What a poor excuse for a vampire, so meek, not at all tyrant as the stories told of the other predecessors, the most pathetic king yet."

"Shut up," I snap at him. "He's not pathetic, nor is he weak!" I snarl, grinding my teeth together, pulling at the chains, I hear the whine and creak, and I continue to strain them.

"You still haven't learnt your place," he sighs, clicking his finger again, returning the flames once more and douse me in a fire, and then disintegrate them, letting my skin patch itself together. "Any last words, boy?" I glare at him before spitting in his face. Thrusting his sword into my torso and igniting a flame in his hand, ready to burn me alive.

The ground before us shakes, the mirror cracks and shatters glass all over the ground. The shadows, the warlock once banished, have risen again, swimming and swirling within the darkness, hearing their little voices talk over each other, like a jumbled mess, unable to decipher who is speaking and what they are saying. The house violently shakes, bricks falling from the high ceiling, shattering as they hit the stone ground, nearly missing the Warlock's head. He struggles to stand on his own two feet, stumbling backward, almost falling onto his bottom. A hand slaps onto the warlock's throat, sharp claws wrapping around his delicate skin, gently putting pressure against the soft flesh and cutting him slightly. The flames die out, his eyes bulge out from his head, his back arches trying to relieve the pressure on his neck. I smile, knowing whose hand it belongs to.

"How dare you lay a hand on my son," Syrus snarls, two snake-like fangs puncturing his throat, dragging them across his skin, tearing deep into the flesh and guzzling every drop of his blood. The shaking stops, the building is stable once more, and the shadows calm and dull themselves to a whisper, cheering their master on. The air feels heavy, every part of my being screams to bow down, to respect our king. It took me every fibre of being to ignore it. Syrus drops the body, it falls with a thud, and it leaves little blood pools out onto the floor. Syrus kneels down, snaps the cuffs around my wrists, and I wrap my arms around him, embracing him into a hug.

"I-I thought you would never wake," I murmur, tears streaking down my face.

"I had some help," Syrus laughs a little.

"Your—your shadows they -," I cut myself off and begin trembling like a leaf.

"I know, it's ok, they disappear and re-appear all the time. Quite annoying," Syrus explains, and I shake my head.

"They protected me," I mumbled into his shoulder.

"Guess they like you," Syrus chuckles, finding this more amusing than I. My eyes land on the body of the man who supposed to raise me and love me. Only to lie in a pool of his own blood. A small shadow secretes from the ground, bowing to us and then disappear. His soul will forever bound to Syrus's will, a fitting punishment for a man who is so arrogant, believing he was untouchable. No grandstand, no epic battle. His cockiness and arrogance became his greatest downfall.

"Father," I whisper, testing the waters. "Can we go home?" I ask, wincing a little, waiting for his reaction. Syrus pulls back and smiles at me.

"Of course. Let's go home, my son," Syrus repeated, the tears didn't stop when I hear the word, the one thing I always wanted in the world, a father who loves me, a family, a home and I finally have it.

Home repairs for dummies

When I agreed, to be known as the son of the vampire king, I didn't expect to have to repair windows or making them watertight for the impending rain that will fall in the future. I only stare at and glass-less frame and blankly stare at the shattered glass on the ground. The only solution is boarding the window with wood and getting nails and the tools, which can take some time. Unless I kill someone for their house, a new home would be lovely, one made from stone . . . or windowless.

"I'm back!" I look up from my pondering mind and see Syrus carry large planks of timber, a hammer in hand and . . . no nails.

"Where did you get those?" I asked him. Syrus places the timber down and digs the nails out of his pocket. I sigh in relief, thanking some unknown god for the bits of iron.

"Stole them," he simply replies and hands over the pile of nails into my hands.

"Instead of stealing materials, couldn't we just find a new house?" I asked Syrus and watched him pick up the plank and hold on to one end and expect me to hold the other end.

"Probably, but do you have a place in mind?" he asks me.

"A place without windows," Syrus snorts out a laugh and goes back to nailing the board. Out of the corner of my eye, I notice the second window had spiderweb crack throughout the glass. I sigh to myself, taking note. We may have to board that in the future.

"I'm sure this isn't how you expected on your first day back home," Syrus adds, nailing the other end, and I pass him one nail at a time.

"Well, we weren't expecting you to shatter glass with your mind as you got frustrated with a book you read. It gives away your emotions," I reply, giving him a cheeky smile. "No longer do I have to guess. I can just watch the glass," I giggle, and Syrus grunts out.

"Until I learn to control it," he responds, picking up another plank. "Or . . . I might not," Syrus whispers to himself. "What if I can't control it . . . what if I am unable," the glass panes cracks spread before shattering once more, jolting Syrus from his thoughts. He sighs to himself and investigates the second broken window. "This is going to be a problem," he sighs.

"We could live in a cave till you control it," I suggest, hoping to get a smile from the vampire, but he stares at the glass solemnly. "Or not," I murmur. Syrus snaps out of his thoughts and blinks in acknowledgment.

"Sorry, " he murmurs. I shrugged it off and walked over to the planks of wood.

"C'mon, let's finish it before it does rain," I smile and pick up two pieces. Syrus gives a small smile and nods.

***

The windows look good . . . well as boarded windows look. Syrus not so much. He's scared, unable to gain control of this new power, unable to grasp its capabilities, let alone being able to feel anything, without breaking another window, but we both know that will happen again. Already I can see the window next to him begin, as his panicked thoughts overwhelm him.

"You're cracking the glass," I murmur, and Syrus snaps out of his thoughts. Clearing his throat, he sits back and takes an unneeded breath, mumbling an apology. He stares at the ground, tilting his head to the side, and hums. Syrus focus's on his left side, looking out of the corner of his eye, yet there is nothing there. It's slightly unnerving, as I don't know exactly who he is looking at. "What . . . did they say?" I ask, my voice a little shaky.

"There's a kingdom in the far east," Syrus stops and pays close attention to the voice in his ear. "Past the snow," he trails off.

"Far east?" I questioned, and Syrus nods.

"They might teach me how to control this power," he murmurs.

"Ok, how do we get there, do we walk?" I asked him, but he remains in place, like a solid stone statue.

"I can flit through the shadows, but I don't want to leave you behind. It would take us months by foot, and there is nothing to eat out there. We would struggle. Animal blood can make us sick if we have too much," Syrus summarises before sighing and throwing his face in his hands. I get up from the floor and wrap my arms around the stressed vampire.

"We'll figure it out." Syrus eases up and hugs me back.

"I know," he sighs and let's go, but knits his brows together once more. "A door? What door?" he asks the air. *Door . . . I remember that term.* "And how do we find this door?" Syrus growls, and the smallish shadow appears from the darkness.

"His grimoires spoke of a door," I murmur, looking at the shadow, knowing who they once resembled. "A door to another world, but only witches and warlocks are born with the sight, to protect the balance. I could never see them but he could," I whisper, watching the small shadow creep back into the darkness.

"It's not him anymore," Syrus snaps me from my thoughts. "It contains his knowledge but none of his memories, feelings, thoughts. The soul doesn't know who you are, all it knows is I am his master and nothing else," Syrus assures me.

"It's rather fitting, to have him serve you for all eternity. An appropriate punishment for a proud warlock even if he is a shell of his former self, unbeknownst that he became something else," I murmur my eyes still trained on the dark corner.

"It is," Syrus whispers.

We both stayed silent till we hear a knock on the door. We both look at each other, sniffing the air for a scent, nothing, not even a heartbeat. Syrus is the first one to move to the door and open it. A long spindly shadow stands before us, carrying three large, leather-bound books.

"Well . . . that's convenient . . . those would be the grimoires," I murmur, staring at the creature dumbfounded. Syrus sighs and slouches forward.

"I told you they do their own thing from time to time."

"It's . . . helpful," I add, taking the old books from the shadow, awkwardly thanking it afterwards. Placing the books on the table in the far corner of the room, Syrus grabs one volume, and I grab the other. We both began scouring through the old yellow pages, with nearly ineligible handwriting but legible enough to decipher what they are talking about.

"Found it," Syrus call out. I look over my shoulder as he comes back to the table. I notice the sun is rising over the horizon from the window. *Did we read all night?* "There's a symbol, only those who tie to Mother Nature can see them. They can give the sight to others, but we need a member of the magical community to receipt the spell," Syrus reads out. I furrow my brow, vaguely remembering I had once read the passage a long time ago. Doors are gateways to other worlds and places within worlds where there is a door present we can step through it.

"So once we find a witch where we will go?" I ask. Syrus gives me a warm smile and closes the book.

"Where ever we want, but first we need to go to the Yamato kingdom," Syrus declares.

"What's in there and where is that?" I ask incredulously.

"Don't know, but they have methods that can help or so I'm told," he smiles, leaving the room. "C'mon now, let's get ready. We have a witch to find!" I sigh, slowly getting up from my seat and shaking my head but smiling none the less. This certainly will be an exciting adventure.

Mending relations

Syrus had heard rumours of wandering Vikings within the mountains, travellers feared them, priests exorcised them, hunters and knights kill them. These Vikings are not ordinary, no. Every single one is part of the magical community, travelling the lands and gathering more of their kind, other Viking clans happily gave them up or fought to the death to keep them, but in the end, they all have a target on their backs. To religion, magic is the devil's work, to those who follow faith, magic is a sin. It's funny, both species hated by humans just as much, but because of bad blood, we will never get along.

None of this agreed with me, but it was our only choice. Carrying a backpack with the old grimoires, and we walk along the stone path, cutting through the face of the rock. I hear we are indestructible and a fall would not kill us, but this is not something I would like to test. I look down at the misty forest and swallow my fear and cling closer to the face of the mountain.

"Rune," I look forward and see Syrus is further along the trail, calmly standing there as he waits for me. "You'll be fine, one step at a time, and if you fall, don't worry, you can't die from this," he yells across the empty valley.

"Is that supposed to help me!" I yell out, my voice echoes into the empty void. I still cling to the rock face, slowly taking side steps like a crab.

"Yes—it helps me, I've fallen from many cliffs in my time!" Syrus shouts, his voice travelling through the mist and spiralling down to the abyss below.

"Not helping!" I shout, scuttling along, feeling my heart beat once more. It was only another five more minutes before I am on more stable ground and wrap my arms around the vampire. Shaken a little from our brief climb. "I don't want to climb anymore," I sniffle.

"You don't have too, we're on the top of the range, solid ground from now on," he soothes, patting my head. I nod into his chest and finally let go, my nerves still getting the better of me.

Syrus led, and I followed, mist blanketing the ground. It slowly sinks to the floor, making it hard to see any twining or exposed roots. We took one step at a time, carefully feeling around with our feet with each step, testing the solid earth. The light in the forest slowly grows dimmer, we both dive deeper and deeper within. I remain vigilant, listening to every sound, counting every step, and breathing in any scent I could pick up. My hands shook, desperate to grip onto something, I snag the hem of Syrus's shirt and pull myself closer to him.

"Do you really think they are here?" I whisper, clinging on tighter to the older vampire.

"If the rumours are correct, then hopefully yes," Syrus gives a quick reply and continues forward. Does this vampire fear nothing?

I jump around, hearing a sharp snap behind me, scanning the dark woods, listening for any sign of life. Swallowing the fear down, reminding myself I am the monster to go bump in the night. I am the most fearful creature. "Rune," I jump again and see Syrus a few metres away from me. "Are you coming?" Syrus confirms. I nod my head, running back to his side, clinging to his shirt once more. I hear another snap, quickly hugging Syrus and we both stop. "Did you hear-." My sentence cut off when the trees come to life, Syrus ripped out from my arms, roots tangling around my feet, and wrapping around my wrists tightening their hold and throwing me to the ground.

"You all right?" Syrus shouts. I look up and see the vampire hang from above.

"Yeah," I breathe through the panic. "You?" I swallow the non-existent spit from my mouth.

"Oh you know, just hanging around," he quips, I snort, hiding my face. I can't laugh, can't laugh.

The forest illuminates a light green glow. The men and woman come out from the darkness, brandishing sharp hatchets and broadswords, arrows aimed at Syrus and some directed to me. One Viking is chanting, shielded by his brethren some, some hold balls of flames in the palms of their hands ready to set us aflame in a moment's notice.

"Syrus," I call out.

"We're going to be ok," Syrus assures me, but I don't feel so assured looking at the powerful Viking mages.

"Only fools who climb the mountains come looking for us," a voice booms from the dark. A tall, broad man comes out from the darkness, clawed scars trail across his face, starting from his right cheek, scaring his lips and ending at his chin. His shoulders back, his broad chest puffing out, making him look more intimidating. "Yer surrounded, I suggest you give up and accept your fate."

"I think you need to look again," Syrus states calmly. The chieftain looks to his clan. The shadow creatures Syrus controls have already made their move. Sharp talons wrapping around their necks, weapons taken away, and the shield guards taken down, and the warlock is no longer chanting. The chieftain glares at me, already dropping his own weapon to the ground.

"So the rumours are true, you have returned," he sighs. "What do you want, leech?" he asks.

"A trade, we have some grimoires, full of knowledge, probably some of us to you and in trade, you give us the sight," Syrus negotiates. The chieftain chuckles, shaking his head and looking up to meet Syrus's eyes.

"You know who you are dealing with. We're Vikings, we destroy creatures like you," he reminds us.

"But your warlocks and witches first. If you follow the magic of mother nature, you answer to her," the chief looks away and stares at his people.

"Yet you hold us by the throat with your . . . things," he grunts.

"You attacked first!" I snap, baring my fangs at him. The chief laughs louder. Walking closer to me, I struggle in the root's grip, fear kicking in, baring my fangs like a trapped animal, trying to remain ferocious.

"You got balls, boy," he chuckles. Reaching for the backpack and grabbing the books. I struggle against the roots. Feeling them getting weaker with each tug. He flicks through the old grimoire, his smile faltering with each yellowed page he turned.

"Never thought I'd see the day," he breathes. "Is the warlock truly dead, the one who used Decay magic?" he asks, snapping the book shut.

"It's a bit of a story," I answered. The chief nods, muttering a few words under his breath, and the roots slowly retract. Letting go of my hands and feet, I slowly get up and brush the dirt off me. Syrus is back to the floor, I run to him and hug him tight. All the shadows disappear back into the darkness, ready to defend their master when needed.

"Sigurd."

"Syrus." Both men nod to each other.

"Our community owes you a great deal of gratitude. Those who use decay magic turn their backs against Mother Nature. Dangerous to all walks of life." Syrus nods and remains silent. Sigurd nods and turns to his people, signalling them to move. Syrus follows the signal and trails behind. I swallow my fear and stay close to the older vampire if something goes wrong, I know I can rely on him to protect me.

Sunrise

This doesn't sit well with me, I've been continually looking over my shoulder for the last two days, ready for them to pull a sneak attack. Thankfully, they have been keeping their distance, not wanting to mingle with two vampires. I swallowed the dread and went along with the plan, much to my dismay. We explained what went down, Syrus could sense my distrust placed with the magical community, leaving out certain pieces to my origins. Syrus does not blame me, he understands at least.

"I don't trust this," I murmur to him as we patiently sit in Sigurd's home.

"I know," Syrus murmurs. "But we have no other way unless you want to go trekking through ice and snow for months," Syrus smiles at me, trying to make light of the situation.

"They hate us . . . just because we killed . . . that bastard, doesn't mean they will keep their word," I say with haste just before Sigurd walks in. Flexing his burly arms as he stares at us lanky vampires. He could snap a log in half, crush rocks between his thighs, and hurl axes over mountains and with magical abilities, he would be a formidable foe to face.

"A deal is a deal," he grunts looking at me. I shrink under his gaze, quickly leaning to Syrus for comfort. "You told me what happened, have been civil within my clan and did Mother Nature a favour, I will give you the sight," he says and hobbles over to his workbench. Grabbing materials, herbs and powders around him, a wooden to mix in, he hums as he goes around, making the concoction. "I can understand your mistrust," he blurts out, and I jump in my seat. "We all have a story to tell for mistreatment. You both lost a lot because of deranged and crazy warlocks hyped up on decay magic . . . but we're all not like that," he says and pricks his finger, dabbing the blood into the potion.

"We prefer natural, using the magic Mother Nature had given us what she intended for us. Decay magic is to take lives and use the dead for power." He turns to us with the wooden bowel in his hand. "I am sorry for what you both went through. It's not enough, but I hope maybe . . . our species can patch things over," he says sympathetically. Syrus stands up with a small smile.

"One day. . . but for now, we have plenty of issues to deal with within our species," Syrus puts his hand out, and Sigurd takes it. "But let today be a start," both shake, nodding to each other with a smile reflecting one another. My mouth drops slightly, surprised to see how forgiving he is.

Sigurd puts the potion in Syrus's eyes first, chanting the spell and then me, expecting burning agony, or sharp stabbing pain. I feel nothing, except one thing.

"I can't see," I panicked, quickly getting up from my seat and stumbling over my feet.

"That will last half a day," Sigurd assures, but I didn't believe him.

"Sure, and now my sight has gone forever," I replied smartly.

"Don't get smart with me, lad," he huffs banging the bowel, making me jump ten feet in the air. I hear Syrus sigh and gently take my hand.

"It will be alright," he whispers assuringly. I nod my head but realise he can't see me.

"I know," I croak.

***

He wasn't lying. Our vision came back within half a day, and by the next morning as the sun broke the horizon, we left the camp, Syrus thanking everyone for their help and hospitality. I stayed far away, feeling uneasy to interact with them, sceptical of their kind nature. Vikings aren't naturally kind to strangers—plus all of them being magic users, this doesn't make it any better. They hate vampires . . . or have a distrust of them, just as we have a distrust of them.

We walk side by side down the mountain track, searching for the symbol Sigurds has told us to look for. I look to Syrus, a small smile gracing his lips as he looks forward, the rising sun blaring in our direction.

"Why did you say those things?" I ask, finally breaking my frustration. "You know what they are capable of, they could have killed us." I hissed, feeling my fangs press up against my upper lip.

"The mages we faced are dead," Syrus says and looks at me. "Hate can only lead to more hate. Casting judgement on others from the actions of individuals can only lead to more death," Syrus explains. I knit my brow together, unhappy with this answer.

"You lost so much because of a warlock, so did I. Why trust them?" I ask.

"I understand your pain, what you went through is inexcusable, I don't expect you to get over it in a day, and

I'm not asking you to like them either," Syrus sympathises. "The warlock I dealt with has been dead long ago. The anger and hatred I felt slowly left as the years went by, but the difference is choosing to let the pain go and look forward to the future," Syrus advises me, gently placing his hand on my shoulder.

"Shouldn't you be following your own advice," I tease, giving him a fanged smile? Syrus tsks and laughs.

"Probably, but I rather help those I care about than myself," Syrus shrugs. "And besides, if we want to move forward as a species, having an ally can't hurt," Syrus smiles.

I shake my head, looking forward down the mountain. A little symbol appears, glowing on the rock face. My mouth drops open and grabs Syrus's attention. We both move closer to the symbol, both unsure if we should use the words to open the door or stare at it a bit more.

"You ready?" he asks me.

"Ready when you are, Father," I urge, giving him the biggest smile I could muster. Syrus smiles back and turns his attention back to the door.

"Let's go, my son."

Social Media

Facebook: www.facebook.com/belindatopan

Twitter: twitter.com/BelindaTopan

Instagram: @belindatopan

Books

Living With Vampires:
www.amazon.com.au/dp/B0842F1GK7

Sunset:
www.amazon.com.au/dp/B08SGF4BRM

ILLUST BY PUPPYPAWW